BELOVED BY

Doms of Destiny

Chloe Lang

MENAGE EVERLASTING

Siren Publishing, Inc.
www.SirenPublishing.com

A SIREN PUBLISHING BOOK
IMPRINT: Ménage Everlasting

BELOVED BY BROTHERS
Copyright © 2014 by Chloe Lang

ISBN: 978-1-62741-125-7

First Printing: April 2014

Cover design by Les Byerley
All art and logo copyright © 2014 by Siren Publishing, Inc.

Printed in the U.S.A.

PUBLISHER
Siren Publishing, Inc.
www.SirenPublishing.com

DEDICATION

My sister Lisa has always been there for me whenever I need someone to talk to or a shoulder to cry on.

Thank you for your love and support.

BELOVED BY BROTHERS

Doms of Destiny, Colorado 6

CHLOE LANG

Chapter One

Phoebe Blue's cell buzzed. Being in a hurry, she didn't take the time to look at the caller ID. "Hello?"

"Hey, baby."

Though she'd heard the sickening voice a million times, she still didn't recognize whose it was. The freak masked his identity with some kind of technology, causing his words to sound monstrous.

"Stop calling me," she told the bastard. How many times would she have to change her number? *At least one more.*

"Phoebe, don't be that way. You know how I feel about you."

"Who are you?" Her heart was racing, and her palms were sweating. *I hate this.*

"The one who loves you with all his heart. I know you feel the same way about me, too. I'm sure you can't wait to feel my dick in your pussy. I have it all planned."

How could anyone be this sick? "I don't fucking know who you are. Why can't you leave me alone?"

"Because you mean too much to me. Have fun at the party, baby."

The line went dead, and she threw the phone down. Should she even go tonight? The guy knew she was going to a party. What else did he know? Would he be there, watching from the shadows?

Shaking from head to toe, she stared at her old ballerina outfit on the bed. God, how long had it been since she tried it on? Before law school, at least. Would it even fit?

As usual, she was running late. The O'Learys' Halloween party had to be in full swing already—the reason for the selection of her old dance clothes as a costume. She'd forgotten to get something else, being so tied up with the Steele case. She loved being an attorney most of the time, but the hours sometimes weren't the best.

She glared at the phone, taking deep breaths to calm her nerves. "You will not dictate to me where I go, asshole." Her words were strong but her insides were still a wreck.

What if he's just outside my door?

"I am stronger than that." She shook her head. The bastard had never shown up anywhere after all this time. He kept his stalking to the phone. "He's a coward. I will not let him win."

Him? If she just had a face, a name…anything, then she could confront the son of a bitch. But she didn't.

She grabbed her brush and looked in the mirror. She'd thought about wearing her hair up like she normally did. It would be appropriate for a ballerina. But she decided to leave it down. In the courtroom, she kept her long brown locks up. At parties, she wore it down. The O'Learys' Halloween Gala was one of the biggest parties in Destiny. *Hair down tonight, ballerina or not.*

When her cell buzzed again, she jumped. This time she looked at the caller ID. *Not the stalker.* "Hey, Ashley."

"Did he call again, Phoebe? I saw a blocked number show up."

All her calls, e-mails, and texts were also routed to Ashley. They'd set it up long ago to make sure everything got logged in on the calendar and so that she could record all Phoebe's hours for billing. After the stalker issue popped up, it gave Phoebe a little comfort to know Ashley was aware anytime the stalker contacted her.

"Yes. He's nothing but a chickenshit, Ash. No worries."

"But I am worried. You need to tell Jason about this."

"He already knows. Remember he took my last cell phone."

Jason Wolfe never left Phoebe's thoughts for more than an hour. He made her crazy—Jason and his two brothers, Mitchell and Lucas, but especially him. She'd fallen hard for them. *That's just water under the bridge, Phoebe.* There was no going back, no rekindling of old flames. Couldn't be. Not after all that had happened with Shane.

"Jason doesn't know about this latest call, Phoebe. He's here at the party. You need to talk to him."

Phoebe didn't want to talk to him. Jason was the reason Shane, her brother, had gotten the book thrown at him for a minor drug possession charge. Mitchell and Lucas had told Jason about Shane's slipup. She might've forgiven all of them if they had come to her first. But they hadn't, probably because she was such an amazing defense attorney. She still didn't understand why Shane had refused to let her defend him, choosing to represent himself instead. Likely he was ashamed of what he'd done, bringing a dark cloud on the Blue family name.

"Should I come over and get you?" Ashley asked.

"No. I don't need a chaperone, Ash. I'm perfectly fine." Even as she said the lie, she continued to tremble. She lifted the white garment up to her body. It would have to do if she was going. She could hear the band fire up through her cell. *Mitchell's band.* Lucas would be there, too. God, it was hard seeing the three Wolfe brothers together anywhere—a rare occurrence since Mitchell and Lucas were still angry with Jason about the breakup with her. "I'll be there in ten minutes. If I'm not, you can come looking for me," she added with a false giggle. Her mind drifted to the happier times she'd had with the three handsome brothers.

"You look gorgeous, Phoebe," Jason said.

She leaned into him. "We don't match. I'm dressed as an angel and you're a devil."

"Kind of backward, if you ask me." Lucas grinned and grabbed

her hand.

"I can be quite the devil when need be, mister," she teased. "Do I need to be one tonight?"

"You're always a little devil, baby, and I love it." He kissed her. "We should've coordinated our costumes. Look at me and Mitchell. I'm Michelangelo and he's Elvis Presley. We don't fit your outfit at all."

"But you do fit me, Lucas. You and Mitchell fit me perfectly." She loved these three with all her heart.

"I get why Mitchell picked Elvis. Everything is about music for him. But your costume choice confuses me. Why Michelangelo?" Jason put his arm around both his brothers. "He's an inventor, painter, and sculptor. That's a departure from what you usually wear to the O'Learys' Halloween party."

"Bro, he was an architect as well," Lucas said. "He's responsible for the dome of St. Peter's Basilica."

Mitchell asked, "At the Vatican?"

"Makes sense to me now why Lucas chose to impersonate the man," Jason said.

Lucas nodded and smiled. "This is our last year together before you go off to boot camp, Jason. You're going to make a great Marine. I still wish we could've done something together for our costumes tonight."

Phoebe took a deep breath, wondering how she would be able to survive without one of her three Wolfe brothers.

Jason's gaze landed on her, and she knew he was seeing right into her like he always could. "You think I won't be coming back for the O'Learys' parties? You and my two brothers can't get rid of me that easy. Costumes that match or not, everyone in town knows we are meant for each other. Yes, it will be hard to be away from you, but I will come back. Soon, the three of you will graduate and head off to college. Well, maybe you and Lucas. I expect Mitchell to take his band on the road.

"Damn right."

"With your talent, I wouldn't expect anything else." Jason *stepped right in front of her and touched her cheek. "I love you, Phoebe Blue. My brothers love you. Nothing will ever change that."*

"I love you, too. I love all of you."

He, Lucas, and Mitchell kissed her, causing her toes to curl.

"Phoebe, are you still there?" Ashley asked, pulling her back into the here and now.

She took a deep breath, pushing the memories away. "I am. I'll be there in ten minutes."

"If you aren't here in five, I will bring the posse," Ashley said firmly, making her feel a little better.

* * * *

Mitchell Wolfe simultaneously hit the snare and symbol, ending the song.

The crowd applauded.

He pulled the microphone toward him. "We are *Wolfe Mayhem* and we'll be back in ten minutes. Thank you."

The Halloween party was a success. He punched the play button of the prerecorded music and stood.

The band's last set made him proud. With the new addition of Godric, the British bass player, to their crew, he could feel them edging closer to his dream. Hank on lead and Big Jim on rhythm were two more perfect fits. He'd been with Hank and Big Jim for eight years. Same with Nancy. Her vocals were amazing, but they didn't quite fit into what he was seeking. Something was missing.

The sound.

God, he'd been hunting for it since the breakup with Phoebe. The search was what had gotten him through the worst of it. His heart was still broken, but he'd learned to put one foot in front of the other. *Or in my case, one stick on the drum after the other.*

"Great set." Godric wore the wolf ears Mitchell had bought his band members for tonight's party. The O'Learys' rule about everyone coming in costume included the band. "Need a cigarette terribly."

"I'll join you." Hank placed his guitar in the stand. "How about you, Big Jim?"

The giant man nodded and turned to Nancy. "I know you can't come with us."

She patted her stomach. "Nope. Not good for my baby."

"What about you, Mitch?" Hank asked. "I know you don't smoke, but we could talk about what we're going to do to find a new lead singer for Denver."

"I'm so sorry, fellows," Nancy said. "I wish I could make it."

"Breaking up the band," Big Jim said with a wink. "The next time I see your husband, I'm going to wring his neck."

"Stop it. I feel bad enough about this," she said. "I wish he could've found something closer, but like it or not, he and I are moving to Texas. He's excited about his new job and about being a new daddy."

"Go smoke, guys. Leave the poor girl alone." Mitchell smiled as Hank and Godric walked away. His mind was spinning about finding a replacement. There were plenty of singers to choose from, but he didn't just want anyone. The band needed someone who would fit in nicely, and he wanted someone who had the talent that would reach what he'd been chasing all these years.

"They love music as much as you," Nancy said.

"And you. I'm going to miss you."

"Me, too. But you'll get a new singer." She put her hand on his shoulder. "Who knows? That might be all you need to get that sound you've been looking for."

"You know me so well, Nancy." He hugged her. "And you're going to make a wonderful mother. What are we going to do without you?"

"You'll get by. Mamas have to leave the nests."

"I thought it was the mama birds who pushed their babies out of the nest, not the other way around."

"Like I could get you, Hank, and Big Jim to leave any nest of mine," she teased.

He was five years older than Nancy, but she'd always taken care of the band. "I will miss you."

"You're going to find your sound, Mitch. I know you will. I was holding you back."

"Don't say that. You're a wonderful singer."

"I think I'm pretty good, but it is true that my voice didn't quite fit where you needed it to be. Hank and Big Jim are amazing. I saw you smile when Godric hit that riff on his bass tonight. You're so close. I know you will find it soon."

"I hope so." He recalled when the sound had first come to him. It had been under the stars next to Phoebe.

On a secluded part of Lover's Beach, Mitchell gazed into Phoebe's eyes.

They'd made love for the first time. He held her close, enjoying the feel of her skin next to his.

"I love you, baby."

"I love you, too," she whispered.

There was so much he wanted to tell her, but there were not enough words in the entire world to convey how he felt about her.

But the music he heard in his mind expressed every emotion inside him.

That night at Lover's Beach had been the first time he'd heard the sound—*their sound, his and Phoebe's.* But it wasn't the last time. To this very day, whenever he looked at Phoebe, the sound came again. She was still his inspiration.

He missed her, missed how easy and wonderful it had been before with her. He even missed his brothers, but nothing would be the same. Not after all that had happened with Shane.

"You drifted off, Mitchell," Nancy said. "Where'd you go?"

"Remembering the old days. We sure had lots of fun on the road together."

"Right now, you need a singer for the Denver gig. I can call the musician's union for you. I'm the one who dropped the ball on you tonight. I wish I could've given you more notice."

"It's fine, hun. I'll take care of it in the morning." He spotted Phoebe's assistant over Nancy's shoulder wearing a ladybug costume.

"Is she here?" she said, turning around.

"Is who here?"

"Don't even try that with me, Mitchell Wolfe. You know. Phoebe Blue. That's who you keep scanning the room for and the one you were thinking about when you drifted off a moment ago. Old days, right? Don't deny it."

"You should apply for an interrogator's job when you get to Dallas. I'm sure they could use someone with your intuitive skills, kiddo."

"I don't see Phoebe." Nancy looked around the room.

He shook his head. "She's not here, but her assistant is."

"Ah. Ashley. I will never understand why you Wolfe brothers are so thickheaded." Nancy sighed. "Go ask Ashley if Phoebe's coming or not."

"Bossy, much?"

She leaned forward and kissed him on the cheek. "Always."

"Is this you pushing me out of the nest?"

"Something like that. Go. Now."

He walked to the buffet table where Ashley stood. Before he got to her, he heard the most amazing voice. He stopped in his tracks and turned to where the sound came from.

Kaylyn Anderson, Betty's daughter, was singing the last song of the band's set and doing it beautifully. Loading her plate up with fruit and apparently unaware of his presence, she continued to belt out the melody better than he'd ever heard it. *This must be the best-kept secret in Destiny.* He closed his eyes, letting every note flood into his ears. The image of Phoebe Blue floated in his mind.

I've found our sound, baby. This is it. This is really it.

* * * *

Lucas Wolfe stood by the window with the two Ryder brothers—Doc and Mick, both dressed as football players. "Not fair, guys. This is two years in a row you've put on your high school uniforms."

"So?" Mick said. "We still fit in them."

"So do I." He shook his head, looking at his Grecian costume. "At least I put in some effort."

Doc laughed. "A fake beard, white sheet over jeans, and a pair of boots are hardly effort, Lucas. You might be ready for the toga party at Phase Four next week, but I'm certain you won't be bringing home the top prize for the costume party. What are you supposed to be?"

"Not what—who. I am Phidias." He fluffed his gray beard. "One of the most important architects of all time. He oversaw the building of the Parthenon."

"You look great, Lucas." Gretchen didn't stop to add more, but passed by with a tray of delicious snacks. The dear woman was dressed as a character from one of the latest children's animation movies, per usual. This year, she'd gone all out with a blonde wig, white smock, and every inch of her exposed skin was blue.

The three of them gave her thumbs up.

Mick smiled. "She's going to win again this year."

"I think you're right." Doc nodded and then turned to Lucas. "Are you all set for the new clinic's ground breaking?"

"Yes. I finished the model this morning." He loved being an architect. His career was the one thing in his life that made sense and gave him purpose. "It's ready for the big reveal."

"Everyone is going to love it, I'm sure," Doc said.

"How's the Boys Ranch coming along?" Mick asked. "Don't Amber and the Stone brothers want to open it in December?"

"By the number of orphan boys Amber's sister, Belle, is already carting around town, I think it is open now." Doc grinned. "Have you seen how Juan is big man on campus with those five other boys?"

"He's twelve now, going on thirty." Ethel O'Leary walked up, wearing the regal gown of a queen. It suited her. "Juan is quite the paintball player, too."

Mick put his arm around the wonderful lady. "I bet by next year's tourney, he'll come home with a trophy."

"He might win the whole thing," she added.

"I wouldn't doubt it." Doc's tone turned serious. "You are taking it easy?"

She saluted him. "Yes. I'm taking it very easy."

Ethel had gotten a bullet in her leg less than a week ago when Mitrofanov's men had come looking for Jena. The woman had bounced back beautifully.

"I want you sitting more than standing, young lady," Doc ordered.

"Fine. I'm just glad we could have this party." Ethel's eyes welled up. "Everyone has been so sad about what happened to Shannon. The town needed this more than ever."

Lucas agreed. Shannon Day's murder hung heavy on all their hearts. She was a wonderful, eccentric woman. Jason was taking it harder than most since the middle-aged lady had been his dispatcher and all-around go-to gal.

"The first dormitory and barn will be completed December fifteenth," Lucas told them, spotting Jason standing next to Dylan Strange.

Those two were dead set on bringing back Niklaus Mitrofanov to face trial here in Destiny. They remained away from the bulk of the crowd in a corner of the room. Dylan was CIA, a man who got the job done, whatever it took. Jason, Lucas's brother, was the lawman, the everything-by-the-book guy, and the very proud sheriff of Destiny.

"That's great." Ethel smiled. "You should be very proud of all you've accomplished, Lucas."

"I will be when it's completed. We still have a main house, another dormitory, a library, a school, and who knows what else Amber will come up with. The Stone Boys Ranch is going to be a wonderful addition to our town."

"You can say that again," Mick said.

Doc looked at his watch. "Isn't it about time for Patrick's story?"

She nodded. "He's added something that I think the kids are going to love."

"The kids and us," Lucas said, noticing Mitchell by the buffet table.

He wasn't sure why his brother was standing behind Kaylyn with his eyes closed. Not surprising. Mitchell was the dreamer, the musician, the artist.

Lucas didn't understand either of his brothers much. He was more pragmatic, landing somewhere in between the two extremes of his siblings. He could never chase the wind like Mitchell, nor could he stand so rigid when the loss was so great like Jason had done.

The memory of how the three of them had lost Phoebe, all because of the mistake they'd made when it came to her brother and because of Jason's unbending will, colored everything in Lucas's life.

"Sweetheart, you can't mean that," Lucas said, feeling his heart rip apart. Phoebe was the love of his life. He couldn't lose her. How would he survive?

"But I do mean it." She stood in front of him, Mitchell, and Jason. Her arms were folded over her chest.

He could see she was shaking, which gave him a sliver of hope. "Talk to us, baby."

"We can work this out," Mitchell added. "Give us a chance."

Jason didn't say a word. After what had happened at the diner, what could he say?

The doors to the courtroom opened. Shane was led out in handcuffs.

Phoebe wept.

"It's going to be okay, sis," Shane said. "Trust me. I'll be fine."

After Shane and the officers went out the door, she turned to Lucas and his brothers. "We are done. This is over."

The closeness Lucas had once felt with Mitchell and Jason was gone. He and Mitchell had been able to heal some of the hurt, having played the smallest of parts in Shane's undoing and the gulf that had been created in Phoebe's heart, but the bond only held on by a thin thread. The wound between him and Jason was just as deep and fresh as it had been three years ago.

He could imagine leaving his brothers, his mom and dads, and even Destiny—something he never would've thought possible before.

Mitchell started talking to Kaylyn, which surprised Lucas even more. There was something in his brother's manner that didn't quite gel with his demeanor since the breakup. Mitchell seemed almost...*happy.*

* * * *

"Mitrofanov surely doesn't have the five million in cash." Jason looked at Dylan, who was wearing his signature outfit—sunglasses and dark suit and tie.

"Likely he's exchanged it for something more portable, like diamonds or art, but it is certainly still transferable." Dylan continued glancing at his and his brother's lovely wife, Erica, who was standing by the stairs with Cam. She was dressed as Juliet and Cam was dressed as Romeo.

"Nice costumes your brother and wife have," Jason stated, trying to goad Dylan a bit. Of course, he had no room to talk, wearing his sheriff's uniform tonight. *Special dispensation by the O'Learys, thank God.*

Dylan didn't take the bait. Jason liked the guy. Always had. They were similar in many ways, but Dylan could bend rules. Something he could never do.

"The agent replacing Black should be here any minute," Dylan told him. "In my book, no one can take Black's place, but I will work with him just as hard as I worked with Black. I don't know the man, but his name is Brown. Former FBI."

"Is that normal, going from FBI to CIA?"

Dylan shrugged. "Apparently quite the climber. Has connections all the way to the top of the Agency."

Thinking about all the killings in Destiny of late made Jason's jaw tighten. Black was only one of a very long list of victims.

Jason wasn't sure if he would ever get over losing Shannon, but he vowed to bring down the man responsible for her death—whatever it took. He wished he had someone to talk to about all of it. But he didn't. Not anymore. Not since Phoebe. Like it or not, he was an island now. Still, Destiny needed him more than ever. He couldn't let his guard down with anyone, not even the unflappable Dylan Strange. He would work with him but also keep one eye on the man. Spies didn't give much credence to the law, like Jason did.

"How are you, the Texans, and Jena going to deal with the new boss?" he asked.

"You're going to have to deal with him, too, Sheriff. You agreed to be on the team."

"More like the governor agreed for me, remember? That was Black's doing."

The hint of a smile appeared on the stoic man's face. "Yes, it was, but you are on the team."

"Dylan, we will make sure that Black's killer pays."

"I'm glad we're on the same page, Jason. I need you to bring that piece of shit down."

Mitrofanov. Definitely a piece of shit. "What about Kip Lunceford? Have they moved him to the new facility yet?"

"Actually, I believe his ride just left his old prison."

A woman walked in through the door. She wore dark gray slacks and a blazer. Her straight, dark hair was cut short at chin length.

"Either that's the best CIA lady costume around or looks like the new boss isn't a *him* at all, Dylan."

"I see that."

The woman headed straight to them but was intercepted by Megan Stone. Did they know each other?

"The agent is nice looking," he told Dylan.

"You on the market again?"

"Maybe," he lied. He wasn't ready for a relationship with anyone. A tumble in the hay might do him some good, though.

A few steps behind the female CIA agent, Phoebe entered the room. Her long, brunette locks with hints of gold flowed around her shoulders, just exactly how he'd always liked. Still did, though he rarely saw her that way since their breakup. *God, why can't I get past her?*

Jason gazed at Phoebe next to his special tree. She looked more beautiful than ever.

"I can't believe summer is almost over," she said. "Back to school. I'm glad we're all going to be in high school together."

"Me, too, baby."

"You'll be a senior. I bet you get chosen as homecoming king." *She grabbed his hand. "And if you do, I better be your homecoming queen whether I'm a freshman or not. This is Destiny. The queen doesn't have to be a senior, don't you agree?"*

"I think you're getting ahead of yourself. School hasn't even started. Who knows who will be elected king?"

"I know. Everyone loves you. You will win."

He loved her fire. "I'll be sure to campaign my heart out for you, honey, to get you the votes you need."

"Lucas and Mitchell better do the same if they know what's good for them," she said with that smile that always made him so happy. "One more year together before you leave." He saw tears well up in her eyes.

He'd been waiting for the perfect moment to tell her how he felt about her, though he was certain she already knew. She was his world. She was the one he wanted to spend the rest of his life with. Tonight was the time to open his mouth and tell her everything.

He took his senior ring off his finger. "Phoebe Blue, I love you. I've loved you for as long as I can remember. I want you to have this. I want everyone at school and in town to know that you are mine. You are my girlfriend."

Her face brightened as he pulled out a gold chain from his other pocket. "I love you, too, Jason Wolfe. Yes, I will wear your ring."

He pulled the chain through the ring and then put it around her neck. "I will always love you, baby. Always and forever."

He kissed her, the girl of his dreams.

Jason wished he could go back to that very night one more time. But he couldn't. The innocence of the past was gone. The world had turned dark and hopeless.

Now that her deadbeat, criminal brother Shane was back in town, things were about to get even worse. Shane would be reporting to him on a weekly basis as part of his parole. *Fuck.*

Megan nodded and led the new CIA boss to them.

"Agent Strange, I'm Brown." The woman held out her hand to Dylan.

He took it. "Agent Brown."

The replacement for Black turned and offered her hand to Jason. "Sheriff Wolfe."

He shook her hand. "Nice meet you, Ms. Brown. How do you and Megan know each other?"

"Jo and I go back a few years," Megan informed. "She's the one who arrested Kip."

"So that's how you know her." Jason was more impressed by Black's replacement, knowing how slippery Lunceford could be.

Megan nodded. "We've kept in touch ever since. She might be hard as nails on the outside, but Jo is actually quite a good friend."

"Joanne Brown, gentlemen. We can get to the expanded introductions later." Brown's face darkened. "Megan, do you mind giving us a moment. Agency business."

"Not at all, but you promised to have lunch with me tomorrow. I'm holding you to it."

"Of course," Jo said in a typical law enforcement tone. As Megan said her good-byes and returned to her husbands, the agent turned to Dylan. "We have a major problem, guys."

Chapter Two

Moving through the crowd of vampires, ghosts, and other Halloween attendees, Phoebe put on a smile though her insides were still quaking. She wanted to shake her fears that the call from her invisible stalker had ignited, but couldn't.

Ashley ran up to her, carrying her synced iPad. "You okay?"

"I'm fine. Thanks."

"What did the asshole say?"

"Same thing he always says." She took a deep breath and handed Ashley her cell. "You know what to do."

"Yes, but I don't understand how he keeps getting your new cell's information. We are only publishing the office phone number. We've gotten you new phones so many times, but it doesn't work. You need to talk to Jason, Phoebe. We need his help."

"I think you're right. Where is he?"

Ashley pointed. "Over there with Dylan Strange and some woman I don't recognize."

Before she could take a single step to them, the trio left the room. "Whatever they're talking about looks serious. My stalker issue can wait."

"No. It can't." Ashley didn't lower her eyes one inch. The fire in the girl from Nevada had always been something Phoebe admired. They were alike in many ways. "If not Jason, then Mitchell or Lucas. You have to talk to one of them. Now."

Whenever Ashley spoke like this, so categorically emphatic about the Wolfe brothers, Phoebe's heart broke a little bit more.

"Ash, you've got to stop trying to build a bridge back to my past love life." She loved Ashley's never-give-up attitude on everything but this topic. "It's never going to happen."

"I see how you look at the Wolfe men. You haven't stopped thinking about them, no matter what you say."

"Please. Don't. I can't argue this again with you. You, my dear Ash, are a hopeless romantic. Perhaps you should work on your own love life."

Ashley blinked and this time did lower her eyes, which made Phoebe feel like a total bitch. She wished she could take back what she'd said. Her assistant had told her just enough—though very little—about three guys from her hometown. The picture was crystal clear. Things were different there. Very different from Destiny. A woman was supposed to love one man. Only one.

God, that would be simpler, wouldn't it? But that wasn't what had happened to Phoebe. She was still in love with the Wolfe brothers. All three of them. Even Jason. But it could never be. After what he'd done to Shane, how could she ever forgive him? She couldn't. A woman's heart and her head didn't always agree, which was definitely her case. She might not be able to get the Wolfe brothers out of her head, but she wasn't about to let them back into her life.

She took another deep breath. "We need to get back to work on the Steele case. That's our focus, not some damn crackpot stalker. We've got to be in Chicago to depose Harrison Rutledge, Braxton's lead vet."

"That's next week." Ashley slid her finger to turn on her iPad. "I've booked our flights. We'll be staying at The Ritz."

"Not the Four Seasons, like we usually do?" Chicago was a frequent stop for her and Ashley. Some work. Mostly play. Always shopping on the Magnificent Mile.

"It's all booked up. We're only a few blocks away from our favorite street, Michigan Avenue."

"Good job." Once the deposition was done, they would be up to date. In her gut, she knew Rutledge was the key to everything. The case was an oddball one. Braxton Meat Packing was claiming Steele Ranch had sold them hundreds of diseased cattle and given them numerous falsified records. Not possible. She was making a lot of progress on the case, but still had some loose ends to clear up. Hopefully, going to Chicago would help her to finally get to the bottom of the whole thing.

"Phoebe, I need to talk to you," Jason said, surprising her, coming up behind her like a ghost of the past.

"I'll leave you two alone," Ash said. "Besides, I need to refill my plate with more of Gretchen's yummy snacks." When she got behind Jason, she mouthed *tell him about your stalker.*

Ash walked toward the buffet table and Jason stepped up in front of her. God, he was one of the most beautiful men she'd ever laid eyes on. Stetson hat. Dreamy blue eyes and long lashes which women would kill for. She'd run her fingers over his square jaw a million times. She missed touching him, holding onto his broad shoulders. She knew firsthand what was underneath his sheriff's uniform and it was muscled heaven.

Stop it, Phoebe. "What can I do for you, Sheriff?"

"I need to talk to your brother."

"Which one?" she asked, although she already knew.

"Shane," he said in his deep, masculine tone that always got her tingling. "I need to change his parole appointment time for tomorrow. Something has come up. Where is he?"

Of course. It was always about Shane. "I'm not his babysitter. He's a full-grown man who can take care of himself."

"He's a felon, Phoebe. I have to do my job. I don't like this any more than you do."

That would be impossible. "Really? Seems like you love keeping your thumb on Shane to me."

The old bitterness crawled up from the recesses of her mind. *I can never forgive him. Never.* "Anything else, Sheriff Wolfe?"

He sighed. "If you see your brother, I would appreciate it if you would tell him to call me."

"Fine." There was no way she was going to tell Jason about the stalker now. She was too angry to say much more. "If that's all, I want to get a seat for Patrick's tale about his first dragon sighting."

"That's all." Jason turned and headed out of the room without saying good-bye.

Whatever he, Dylan, and the mysterious woman had been discussing seemed pressing or else he would've certainly stayed for Patrick's story.

She recalled when they were just preteens, sitting together and listening intently to every word about the real green dragon—Jason on one side of her, Mitchell on the other, and Lucas standing behind. Her family and theirs believed they were destined to be together. She'd believed it, too, for a very long time. She might live in Destiny, but she wasn't sure that kind of love actually existed. At least not for her and the Wolfe brothers.

Ashley came back up. "Did you tell him?"

She shook her head. "I couldn't. Per usual, all we talked about was Shane."

"Then I'm marching you over to Mitchell or Lucas right now. I will not take no for an answer, boss."

"If I'm the boss, then why are you the bossiest?"

"I'm worried about this stalker even if you're not."

I'm worried, too. "Okay. Where are they?"

"Mitchell is over there by the buffet."

She turned her attention to the table with all the food. When she saw who Mitchell was talking to, her heart sank.

Kaylyn Anderson. The girl was a knockout. Long blonde hair. Perfect figure. Soft gray eyes. Plus, she was so nice. *So freaking nice.*

They would make a lovely couple. Mitchell's six-three frame next to Kaylyn's five-two added to his dominant presence and Kaylyn's submissive demeanor. Imagining them together caused Phoebe's heart to seize in her chest.

How many times have I stared into Mitchell's unusual eyes? God, she loved them both—the left one blue and the right one brown. He could ensnare her with a single glance. Her mother had told them both, when they were still kids, that the two colors meant Mitchell had amazing gifts—magical even. When they were older, he'd discovered that the brown eye was just a freckle on his iris. Nothing special. But Phoebe knew better. The muscled music man with the coal-black hair was very special. *Even magical.*

Kaylyn and Mitchell were laughing together, and she felt jealousy well up inside her like a tornado.

Stop it, Phoebe. He's not yours anymore.

"Boss, you okay?" Ash asked.

"I'm fine." *He's finally moved on. Isn't that what I've wanted for him? For Lucas and Jason, too? Yes—and hell no.*

Ash frowned. "Then what are you waiting for?"

"He's busy. After Patrick's story, the band will have to run another set." She missed sitting in on Mitchell's jam sessions with Hank, Big Jim, and Nancy. Those were some of her most fond memories. Mitchell loved his music, and so did she. "I can tell him later. Where is Lucas?"

"He's sitting with Doc and Mick over there."

Phoebe looked over at Lucas, the middle-born Wolfe brother, and smiled. He was wearing a toga and a fake beard, no doubt portraying one of his favorite architects, Phidias. The Halloween party was the only time Lucas let down his guard and wore something other than a suit and tie in his office, or jeans and a white shirt when he was on site.

"Time to spill the beans about your stalker to him," Ashley stated flatly. "And what a good-looking man to tell, too. All those Wolfe brothers are gorgeous. I can't believe you let them go."

"But I did." Looking at Lucas was making her heart race. Dark, thick hair that she loved running her fingers through. Six-one and chiseled beautifully from head to toe. His mysterious dark eyes never failed to mesmerize her. *At least he's not talking to some pretty girl. Are you losing your mind? Stop it.* "And I will say it again. The topic of me and the Wolfe brothers is off-limits, Ash."

"Fine. Tomorrow we can pick up where we left off. Right now, I'm taking you over to him." Ash took her arm and led her to one of the three men Phoebe couldn't get out of her heart, no matter how hard she tried.

* * * *

Lucas was thrilled to see Phoebe being led by Ashley in his direction. He stood, hoping they would take his seat. All the sofas and chairs were packed. Like always, it was standing room only for Patrick's story.

Doc and Mick got to their feet, clearly spotting the approaching duo, too.

"Ladies." Doc gestured to the sofa. "Have a seat."

"We only need to talk to Lucas for a moment," Ashley said. "Well, Phoebe does."

"Sit," Mick ordered in his most Dom tone. "The seats are for the ladies. My brother and I need to refill our drinks anyway. We'll get a good view of Patrick from the bar."

Doc nodded, and the two Ryder brothers left.

"That leaves three seats," Ashley said with a wink. "Phoebe, you sit in the middle. Lucas, you take the right. I'll take the left."

"Forgive her, Lucas," Phoebe said with the sass he'd always loved of hers. "She forgets who is boss and who is assistant."

"I never forget. I'm in charge. You pay the bills."

"Everyone, please take your seats. Children gather around." Ethel's silver hair was twisted into a bun at the back of her head, perfect for her queen costume. Her blue eyes danced as the seventy-nine-year-old woman smiled down at Destiny's youngest citizens from the bottom of the staircase. The children sat on the floor in front of the microphone and stand that Patrick was about to give his annual speech from. "Our Master of Ceremonies will be down in two minutes."

"More like five." Leaning on one of the dragon statues in the room, Sam O'Leary, brother to Patrick and Ethel's other husband, wore his glasses on the end of his nose. He rubbed his bald head—a clear act of drama for the kids to enjoy. Eighty-five years old, Sam was as much Peter Pan as Patrick, who was a year older. "The man loves a grand entrance."

"Stop it, Sam." Ethel smiled. "But he's right. More like five." She walked back up the stairs.

Ashley sat in the place she'd picked out for herself.

Phoebe shrugged. "Best to let Ash *think* she's in charge." She sat in the middle of the sofa.

Lucas grinned and took the seat next to the woman he loved more than life itself. God, it felt so good to be next to her. Before he could ask her what she needed to talk about, the lights dimmed and mysterious music filled the air.

Fog from hidden machines wafted through the room. *Patrick does know how to put on a show.*

"Good evening, ladies and gentlemen and distinguished little guests on the floor," Patrick's voice came from every corner of the room, a new addition to the annual event and quite an impressive one to boot. "Tonight, I ask you to let your minds drift back to an earlier era when monstrous, glorious creatures roamed the sky, the earth, and the seas. Some say they never were, but I know for a fact that not only did they live long ago on this tiny blue planet—they are still with us, hidden from the nonbelievers, those who refuse to see what is right in front of their faces."

Lucas loved hearing the old man talk about dragons. Everyone did, even Sam, Patrick's brother, though he rolled his eyes at every telling.

Lucas looked over at Phoebe. How long had it been since they'd sat in the O'Leary mansion listening to every captivating word from the Dragon Master of Destiny?

"In my lifetime, I have seen two dragons, in the flesh. Yes, two. Five more, I have seen out of the corner of my eye, appearing as apparitions, wisps of their amazing selves." Patrick emerged at the top of the stairs, wearing his outlandish silver garb and red cape. In one hand was the golden staff he always carried every Halloween and in the other his pipe, allegedly carved from a dragon bone he'd unearthed in an expedition to Peru in the seventies. He looked like a wizard. In Lucas's mind, ever since he was a child, that's exactly what Patrick was.

Patrick lifted the staff into the air, another change from previous speeches, and thunder rumbled from the speakers. The kids screamed.

Lucas looked at Phoebe, her eyes as wide as they were the first time they'd come here as children years ago. He grabbed her hand, and she squeezed back. His heart soared.

"My first encounter was when I was a prisoner of the North Koreans. Yes, children, this eighty-six-year-old man was a soldier. I was a fighter pilot. During one intense aerial battle, my plane was hit and went down." The sound of an explosion filled the air, more of Patrick's new theatrics.

The crowd applauded their approval.

Patrick never broke character, but Lucas could see a twinkle in the man's eyes. He descended down the stairs, hitting his staff on every step.

Boom. Boom. Boom.

"With blood in my eyes from the wound I'd received from the crash, I made my way through the darkness to the river I'd spotted when I was still in the air. But fate was a harsh mistress that night. Gunshots riddled the air around me."

More sound effects amazed everyone. *What a show.*

"I took a hit to my leg, ending the trek to my escape." Patrick lifted up his robe revealing the scar of his battle wound, something that had always been part of the speech.

The children gasped.

Continuing to hold his robe up, Patrick walked to the stand with the microphone. Clearly, he didn't need it since he was wearing a wireless microphone. He'd likely kept the one on the stand so as not to ruin the surprise of the new sound effects.

"That's real?" Juan asked, staring at Patrick's scar.

"Shh," Belle told the orphan, whom everyone knew she loved as if he were her own. The other five boys, early arrivals for the Stone Boys Ranch, sat with them on the floor.

"Belle, it's fine," Patrick said. "Come up here, lad."

Juan leapt to his feet.

When he was right next to Patrick, the old wizard gestured to the wound. "Touch it."

Juan's jaw dropped. "Really?"

"Yes, really."

The boy brought his finger to the scar.

"Yes, it's real, Juan," Patrick said. "It still gives this old man trouble on wintery nights to this very day." Letting go of his robe, he put his arm around the smiling kid. "A round of applause, please, for the very brave Mr. Juan Garcia."

The crowd roared and Juan smiled from ear to ear. One thing about the O'Learys, they adored children.

Juan returned to the floor, next to Belle.

"Where was I?"

"The bad people were about to take you to the cell," one little girl, who had clearly heard the story many times, yelled out.

He laughed, as did Phoebe and several other adults.

"That's right, angel. War is a terrible thing. My enemy had no sympathy for me. I'd taken out many of their brothers, so I understood their cruelty. Several kicks came from their boots and left me broken and without recourse. They took me back to their encampment like a prize turkey for a Thanksgiving meal. Why they let me live, I still don't know, but they did. I was their prisoner for two hundred and seven days."

The sound of a grandfather clock striking filled the room.

Gong. Gong. Gong. Gong. Gong. Gong. Gong.

Patrick paused, allowing the effect of the passage of time to creep into everyone's psyche before continuing on with the story.

"In time, I healed, though the food the enemy gave me wasn't enough to nourish me back fully. Constant fevers consumed me night after night. I dreamed of escape, but sadly, I had no power to break the bars that held me."

"Until the black dragon showed up," the same little girl shouted out.

"Hush, let Mr. O'Leary tell the story, Amy," her mother told her.

"She's right though." Patrick closed his eyes, inhaling from his pipe. The spicy smoke wafted from its bowl in silvery warm circles, up to the ceiling. "The black dragon came to me first in the darkest part of the Korean night. There was no moon. I thought that he was an illusion, brought on by a temperature spike in my body. But he wasn't. He was real. Very real. You may ask yourself, how does Mr. O'Leary know that?"

"How do you know that, Mr. Patrick?" Jena's daughter, Kimmie, asked.

Several of the kids nodded that they were wondering, too. He clearly had them under his spell.

"You are right to ask, Kimmie. Many have. Most doubt my account. But none are able to explain how a malnourished man with a bum leg in the middle of a heavily guarded North Korean prison encampment was able to escape without a sound. No one. But I can. I was there."

"Tell us," Juan said, his eyes wide. "What did the dragon do?"

"Mr. Garcia, the black dragon saved my life. Did you know that their minds are far superior to ours? Their intelligence is stellar, except the purple dragons', or so I've been told by two of their cousins."

"They talk?" Juan blinked several times. The boy was hooked, now and forever, just like Lucas and everyone else. Dragon hunting up in the mountains was definitely going to be on the kid's next outing.

"Yes, Mr. Garcia. Dragons talk, though they find our languages quite rudimentary and coarse. Their language is the most beautiful sound on the planet. Though I understand only a few words, I, like all humans, don't have the vocal capacity to speak it. But for the first time, ladies and gentlemen and distinguished little guests, I have a recording of a few words from their ancient tongue."

The crowd gasped.

"Scott, we're going off script for a moment. I wanted to save this for later, but since the amazing Juan Garcia asked, please fire off number twenty-two."

"Yes, sir." Scott Knight's voice came through the speakers. "One second."

Everyone held his or her breaths, including Lucas. He looked over at Phoebe, who was doing the same. Hundreds of people were packed in the room but the place was as quiet as a tomb.

Then the most amazing sound came through the speakers. Beautiful and chilling. Clicking tones, high and low, tickled his ears, followed by long, deep rumblings. He closed his eyes and imagined the stirring of a sleeping volcano. Clacks came next, fast and furious. Finally a resounding roar, unlike any lion, tiger, or bear could muster. This came from none other than a dragon. Lucas's belief was renewed once again.

The crowd rose to their feet, giving Patrick a standing ovation.

"That, my friends, was captured on my expedition last year in Nepal. We stumbled upon a sleeping green dragon. A baby. It still didn't have its wings. When it stirred, my team vanished out of the cave, leaving me alone with the noble beast."

"Your official count of seeing dragons in their physical form totals three now, doesn't it?" Mitchell asked.

"Yes, Mr. Wolfe. It does."

Another round of applause.

"What about the black dragon?" Juan asked. "What happened?"

"Thank you for getting me back on track, young man." Patrick smiled. "Scott, we're back on script."

"Yes, sir. All set."

"My first dragon sighting." Patrick rubbed his chin. "His statue is in the northwest corner of our town's park. I asked him his name, and he told me. But alas, it is unpronounceable from the human tongue. We talked for several hours. He told me that he'd been watching me since I fell from the sky. I asked him why. He said that my steely determination reminded him of his own hatchlings, all of which had died hundreds of years ago. I call him Father Dragon. He is one of the few black dragons still living in the world. Night after night, he returned to talk to me. My guards slept like the dead, which they'd never done before. I learned later from Father Dragon that he'd flown above, enveloping the air with his breath, which causes humans and animals to fall fast asleep."

The sound of heavy monstrous breathing filled the room.

"I was immune because the night I first saw him was not the first time he came to me. The night before, he sent the whole encampment into slumber, including me. He came to my cell and breathed from another of his seven lungs into me. From then until now, I am immune to the impact of dragon's breath, giving me a special advantage in the search for the creatures. My final night as a prisoner of my enemies, Father Dragon asked me a question that changed the course of my life."

A deep bass voice that reminded Lucas of James Earl Jones boomed from the speakers. "Will you help to save my kind?"

Hell, with the O'Learys' fortune, it just might've been Mr. Jones's voice playing Father Dragon.

"I answered I would. His giant yellow eyes seemed to sparkle.

Then he took one of his claws, which was at least five feet long, and broke my steel bars as if they were toothpicks. He gently lifted me up on his back and he flew into the air, the place I'd only been in a plane before."

The sound of flapping reverberated off every wall.

Patrick ended the tale about how the black dragon saved him, dropping him off just outside an American base camp in South Korea, to everyone's surprise.

"What about the baby dragon, Mr. Patrick? What happened to him?" Kimmie asked.

"The poor thing tried to knock me out with a big blast of hot air. It didn't work, as you know. I was able to calm him down after telling him the story about Father Dragon that I just told you. Knowing a thing about what dragons need, I gave him directions to a lake where he could find all the fish he needed. The beast promised to come to Destiny when it grows its wings."

"A real dragon is coming to see us. Really?" Juan stood up, as did all the other orphan boys.

"Yes, really. It might be twenty or thirty years, but he's coming."

Everyone stood, applauding like mad. This was the best rendition of Patrick's account ever.

"Mark your calendars, my fellow Destonians. A dragon will one day come to our town. I'll be gone, but you better be ready. They need us more than you know."

The lights dimmed.

More applause.

"Keep your eyes up to the heavens. They're coming." Patrick waved and took a seat in the big chair center stage.

All the kids ran up to him with a million more questions. Sam and Ethel helped the kids form a line. In Destiny, Santa Claus had to take a backseat to the Dragon Master this time of year. Luckily for Sam, who played St. Nick at the O'Learys' Christmas party, he got to enjoy the adoration of all the children then.

"Wow, that was amazing," Phoebe said.

"He outdid himself this year for sure." Lucas saw Mitchell's band take the stage. He only had a few minutes to talk before the music would make it hard to hear. "What do you need to talk about?"

Ashley leaned forward and gave Phoebe a stern look. "Tell him everything, boss. All of it."

"I've got this, Ash." Phoebe sighed. "How about refreshing my drink for me?"

Ashley didn't look convinced. "You're only trying to get rid of me so you can sugarcoat the gravity of the call."

Phoebe traced an *X* over her perfect breasts. "Cross my heart. I will tell Lucas everything. I would like to talk to him alone for a second."

"Oh." Ashley smiled. "I see. I will be happy to refill your drink. How about yours, Lucas?"

The girl had spunk. "Thanks, but I'm still working on mine."

"I'll be back and will want an update."

"Go," Phoebe said. "Now."

Ashley saluted. "Yes, ma'am."

As she trotted off, he turned to Phoebe. "What's Ash concerned about? What's happened?"

"I'm not sure I should involve you, Lucas," she stated firmly. "This is my problem not yours."

He clenched his jaw. "Phoebe, don't do this. Whatever I can do to help, I will. Talk to me."

She sighed. "Might as well get right to it."

"Yes, you should." He could sense the worry in her, which didn't sit well with him. She was a strong, capable woman. Whatever had her anxious, he wanted to know. "Tell me."

"The stalker called again. He got my new number."

Son of a bitch. His entire body tensed. "When?"

Phoebe fidgeted with the hem of her ballet skirt. "Right before the party. I'm sure the guy is harmless."

He doubted that. "I thought Jason was on this weeks ago. Why hasn't he found the fucker?"

"I don't know. All the calls come from blocked numbers. He and Dylan put traces on my old cell phone, but the man never called. How in the world he's able to get my new numbers, I don't know."

"Doesn't sound harmless to me." Lucas's blood was boiling. Phoebe might not be his anymore, but she still was his to protect, no matter what their current relationship status. "Tell me exactly what the creep said to you."

"He called me 'baby' like he always does."

His gut tightened. "And?"

"He uses some kind of voice-masking device. He sounds more like a sci-fi villain. I can't recognize who he is."

That was going to make it harder to identify him. "You think you know him?"

"Shouldn't I?" Phoebe shrugged. "Why would he be stalking and calling me if he never met me before?"

Phoebe was the best at deduction in the entire town, which made her the perfect attorney. But with some psycho gunning for her, Lucas wasn't about to let her be alone. "What else?"

"I told him to stop calling, but he wouldn't hear it. He even told me to have fun at the party tonight. How did he know I was coming to the O'Learys'?"

Lucas scanned the room. *Is the bastard here? Is the fucker watching her from some dark corner?* "With everyone in costume, the stalker could be anyone. Time to get you out of here, Phoebe." He stood up and offered her his hand.

Phoebe looked unsure. "Shouldn't we wait for Ashley to come back before we leave?"

And give the creep more time to watch her? No way. "Text her. She always has her cell and iPad with her. She'll understand. Besides, once she learns I'm spending the night at your place, I'm sure she'll be fine with us leaving without telling her."

"You sure are taking a lot for granted, Mr. Wolfe." Phoebe placed her hand in his, allowing him to help her up.

"I'll sleep on your couch, but I'm not leaving you alone tonight. Understand?"

Phoebe gave him a cute salute, like Ashley had done earlier to her. "Yes, Sir."

Chapter Three

Phoebe opened the door to her home.

"Stay here," Lucas said, removing his fake beard and toga, tossing them to a chair. In only his jeans and T-shirt, he looked formidable, ready to take on any attacker. "I'm going to check your place out."

"Why?" she asked, closing the door. "There's no sign of a break-in. I had to use the key. Aren't you being a little overprotective?"

"With you? I can't help being cautious. You stay here," he repeated in the commanding voice she remembered from long ago.

She shrugged. "Okay." She took a seat in her plushiest chair.

Lucas brought out his gun. Like most Destonians, male and female, he was always armed. She peered into her purse at her own weapon, "Lady Equalizer."

Lucas went through her house thoroughly. All three Wolfe brothers had been in the military. He had been in the Army, Mitchell in the Navy, and Jason in the Marines. She'd never asked the three why they'd chosen different branches to serve in. Didn't have to. She had a good idea why. They were so different from one another. The Marines fit Jason to a tee. Rules. Regiment. He loved structure more than any man she'd ever known. Mitchell was drawn to the Navy for the adventure. Lucas, the middle of the three, was a blend of the other two in many ways. The Army had been good to him.

Lucas returned to the living room. "All clear, Phoebe. I checked each closet and under every bed. Nothing. I even made sure every window was locked. They are. The place is secure."

"I really do appreciate this." Her nerves began to settle down some. "So glad we have been able to remain friends."

"You know we are more than friends and always have been. Always will be."

She shook her head. "Lucas, let's don't go there."

"Go where? It's the truth."

She needed to change the subject. "How about a glass of wine?"

"Wine?"

"Oh yeah, you're a dark beer drinker. I remember." She smiled. "I just happen to have a six-pack of your favorite." The truth was, she kept on hand his, Mitchell's, and Jason's preferred drinks. Funny, since they hadn't been to her home since the breakup. Jason's bottle of Jack was three years old, but whiskey never went bad. Lucas and Mitchell were both beer drinkers. Every six months, she threw out the old six-packs and replaced them with new ones. It might've been a waste of money, but it was a practice she couldn't bring herself to break. Now, Lucas was here.

He smiled. "I remember a lot of things, too, sweetheart. You bring your wine. And of course, beer is always great for me, but we are going to talk. We have the perfect opportunity, and I'm going to take advantage of it. Do you hear me?"

"It's been over three years, Lucas. Haven't we said all there is to say?"

Lucas's eyes narrowed. "Just get the wine, Phoebe." His cell buzzed, stopping him from saying more. "Hello."

She headed into the kitchen to get their drinks, hoping to come up with something she could do or say to derail the conversation Lucas wanted to begin. She'd been avoiding the Wolfe brothers since the breakup. It was always hard on her heart whenever she couldn't. For the past three years, she'd kept them at arm's length. It was how she'd been able to survive.

She heard Lucas yelling at the person on the other end of the phone.

"Listen to me, motherfucker, you call her again and you're a dead man." Lucas's rage was evident in every syllable. "I will find you. I will kill you."

Her heart pounded hard in her chest, and she spilled the wine. *The stalker?* Shaking like a leaf, she left their two glasses and walked back into the living room. Lucas glared at his cell in his hand, staring bullets into its screen. It was clear the call had ended.

Oh no. It couldn't be…"Lucas? Was that him?"

He turned to her, his face blood red. "Yes."

"How did he get your number? Why did he call you?"

Lucas walked toward her, taking her hands in his. "I'm not sure how the son of a bitch has my number, but he called me because he knew I came to your house with you. That we were together. I don't think we need to consider the bastard harmless anymore."

Am I really in danger? She'd wondered about that possibility for some time, but every time she did she tried hard to think about something else. "Oh my God. I can't believe this is happening."

Lucas looked her in the eyes. "Phoebe, like it or not, we will not leave you alone until this bastard is caught."

"We?" Could he promise that?

"You know. The three of us—me, Mitchell, and Jason."

She shook her head. "I can't ask you to do this. Besides, how do you know that your brothers would even agree to such a thing?"

"I know and so do you." Lucas stepped closer, pulling her to his chest. "We have a huge barricade to knock down, but our feelings for you have never changed. And I don't believe yours have changed either." He brought his hands up to her face.

She felt heat well up inside her. *God, it has been so long since he's touched me…since I let him touch me.*

"I'm right, aren't I, baby?" He didn't wait for an answer, but pressed his lips to hers.

Her whole body responded to his kiss, but she still pushed him away. "I can't do this, Lucas."

Since the breakup, no man had kissed her, or anything else for that matter. Though her heart was racing and her skin was tingling, she couldn't forget the damage of what they'd done.

"It's okay, baby. Just relax." He stepped back, removing his hands from her face. She instantly missed his touch. "All I want to do is talk. We need to hash everything out. It's long overdue."

He was right, of course, but she wasn't sure this was the right time. "Why now? Let's worry about the stalker issue first. Once that's worked out and the guy is caught, then we can talk as long as you want."

"Same feisty Phoebe I fell in love with. Baby, we're not going to put this off one more second." His commanding tone didn't leave her any room for argument.

Though he and his brothers knew why she'd ended it, they'd never talked about it. For months, they tried to get her to open up, coming over and calling day after day. She'd refused every attempt. She was afraid she would be unable to resist the sexy Dom trio since she was still in love with them.

"Where's my drink, baby?"

Crap. The wine. "I had a little accident in the kitchen. Sorry."

"Nothing to be sorry about." Lucas put his arm around her shoulders. "Let me help you clean up. Besides, you and I both know I'm the better bartender."

She laughed. "I remember you were heavy handed with the liquor, Mr. Wolfe."

"Don't worry, honey. A glass of wine to take off the edge is fine, but we both need to be clearheaded tonight. We have a lot to discuss."

"I know." It was time to put all her cards on the table. He deserved that at least.

As promised, Lucas helped her clean up the mess she'd made. Then he poured them each a new glass of wine. They sat back down on the sofa. He was so close to her that she could feel the heat from his body on her skin.

For a few long sips, they sat in silence.

She took a deep breath. *Now or never.*

They both started to talk at once, stopping after the first word. She waited, and then began again, but so did Lucas.

They laughed.

"You first, sweetheart," Lucas said politely.

Where to begin…"I still don't understand why you turned Shane in for such a small amount of pot. You could've come to me."

Lucas shook his head. "You're protecting him, Phoebe. You and I both know that it turned out to be much more than just marijuana."

"I could've taken care of this—like I just said—if you just had come to me in the first place." Her heart still ached for how everything had gone down with Shane and her three Wolfe brothers. "He needed family."

"Maybe that would've been a better solution, but we did what we thought was right. Everything we did was to protect Shane. When he started acting so strangely, Mitchell and I began to worry. When we found that bag of weed on him during the camping trip, we confronted him. He exploded."

"I know." The awful memories bubbled up to the surface in her mind. "I read everything in his case file. Besides, I was there at the trial. I heard your testimony first hand."

Lucas looked so sad. "Honey, we had no idea it would turn out the way it did. When we found the meth in his glove box two days later, we knew Shane needed an intervention. That's when we went to Jason."

"He was deputy sheriff then." She remembered how proud she'd been of Jason when he'd been sworn in. Soon after, everything had changed. She'd always known how by-the-book he was, but after becoming deputy, the only thing that seemed to matter to Jason were rules and the law. "Why him? Why not me?"

"We planned on going to you after we talked to Jason. Since he and Shane were also friends, we thought he would want to talk to you and your parents about what we'd found, too."

That is what you'd expect a friend to do. But not Jason. "He didn't though, did he? Same old Jason, taking charge of everything and leaving everyone else out."

"Yeah. That's my brother. Without our knowledge, he went straight to Shane. Shane blew up and punched Jason in the face. That's when they really went to blows at your parents' diner."

Phoebe closed her eyes, recalling how upset her mom and dads had been that day. "Why? Shane and Jason had been so close before."

"Best friends." He shook his head. "I don't know why Jason testified so harshly against your brother."

Nor do I. She would never understand it. "I believe his account played a big role in the extreme sentence Shane received. A first offence getting the maximum is unheard of."

"I have a question for you," Lucas said. "Why didn't you represent your brother? You're the best defense attorney in the state. That didn't make sense to me or Mitchell."

"Shane refused my help." She never understood that either. God knew she had wanted to help Shane. "No matter how much my parents, my older brother, Corey, and I tried to convince him to let me represent him, Shane wouldn't give in. Corey tried to help, too, using whatever pull he had as a US marshal, but Shane didn't want any of us to lift a finger. Not me. Not Corey. Not my parents." Phoebe sighed, feeling the old weight return. "We lost Shane. I didn't know what to do to get him back."

"It's so weird. One day, Shane was the same old fun-loving guy I'd always known and the next day he was a stranger."

"Drugs, Lucas." She hated to think about how they'd changed her brother. "He got caught up in the drugs."

"Phoebe, it just doesn't add up. I still find the whole thing so hard to understand."

"Me, too." She wasn't about to dredge up that the search of Shane's place had found even more drugs and tons of cash. Though her brother had never been convicted of selling, it sure appeared that he must've been.

"I still can't believe this all happened with Shane. I'm sure there is so much more to this than has come to light."

"I believe that, too." She sighed, feeling the weight of the past three years on her shoulders. "But what could that possibly be?"

"I know it has broken your family in two." He touched her cheek. "And it's broken your heart, baby."

She turned and looked into Lucas's loving eyes. "I've missed this, Lucas. You can't imagine how much."

"But I can, baby. I've missed you."

"I wish we could start up where we left off. I want to. I really do. You being here means the world to me, but after all we've been through, I can't see how we can begin again."

He moved his hand to the back of her neck. "But I can. Shane is back. He's served his time. We all need to pull together to make sure he doesn't slip up again. You need me. You need Mitchell and Jason, too."

She shook her head. "Even if that's true, and I'm not saying it is, you guys barely talk to each other these days. I feel responsible but don't know what to do about it. How can you guys help me when you can't help each other? Everyone in town can see you aren't as close as you once were."

"Honey, that's for me and my brothers to work out. Yes, we do have much to discuss, but you aren't responsible for any of our issues. Shane is like a brother to me, Mitchell, and Jason. Corey, too. With all of us in Shane's corner, we can make sure he never has to leave Destiny again."

"Shane does need everyone to help him get back to his old self." Who better than her family and her three Wolfe men to take part in making sure he did? "Where do we begin, Lucas?"

"One step at a time, baby. That's where. We'll figure what Shane needs from us along the way. It's not something you can plan for. Tonight, I want to talk about you. About you and me. The past needs to stay in the past. What I'm asking is for another chance, Phoebe. We had a dream once—a dream about the future that you, me, Mitchell, and Jason wanted. We can have it again."

She leaned her head into his shoulder. "I want to trust you."

"Then do it."

"Help me," she said with tears welling up in her eyes.

She felt him tug on her hair, one of his Dom moves from long ago that never failed to get her attention and make her warm. Like magic, it did the trick.

"I remember your safe word, sub. Do you?"

"Yes, Sir."

"Say it for me now, so I can be sure you do."

"My safe word is…" she hesitated, feeling the gravity and power of that single syllable that she and the Wolfe brothers had settled on during her first training session, "…*freeze*."

"Very good. And your word to let me know your approaching a limit?"

"*Caution.*"

"Right again, sub." He smiled. "On your feet. Time to get you out of that ballerina costume."

"Yes, Sir." She trembled as her desires, which she'd kept in check for three years, began to burn blisteringly hot inside her.

Lucas stood and took his time removing her clothing. One thing about him she always remembered, he never rushed. There was a kind of madness in his unquenchable lovemaking, but there also seemed to be a method.

He flagrantly scanned her body, as if he had a claim to it. In her heart, she knew he still did, even after all these years. She could see the hunger in his eyes, which added to her own excitement.

Once she was down to only her bra and panties, he kissed her wickedly, sending his tongue past her lips. She melted into his kiss, feeling safe again for the first time in years.

As he continued devouring her mouth, Lucas's hands moved up and down her body, probing and pinching her into submission.

He unclasped her bra, pulled it off, and sent it to an empty chair with a toss. His thick fingers massaged her breasts, causing her pussy to burn and her clit to ache.

God, this feels so good, so right. She'd forgotten how her body responded to his manly manipulations. Long dormant nerve-endings were stirring.

Lucas kissed her neck, sending a shiver up and down her body. As he moved his hands to her sides, her skin heated up even more.

She felt his fingers latch onto the waist of her panties. Then he shoved them to her ankles. He stepped back and sent her the most possessive Dom smile she'd seen in years.

"Very good." Then his smile turned into a frown. "You still shave your pussy. Why?"

She gulped, recognizing his tone of jealousy. "Sir, it was something I couldn't give up even after our breakup. No one has touched me since," she confessed, unable to hold back anything from him now that they were in play. Apparently, her submissive side remained under the surface all these years.

As he removed his belt, she gasped. He definitely was still one of her three Doms. The Wolfes would always be the Doms who owned her heart.

He wrapped her wrists together with the leather strap, and she felt her whole being settle into that familiar space she'd missed every second of every day and night—especially the nights—since their breakup.

"On your knees, sub," he commanded.

She obeyed instantly, lowering her eyes as he and his brothers had taught her. *This is where I belong. At his feet. At least for tonight.*

"You are mine, Phoebe Blue. That's never changed."

She saw his T-shirt fall at her feet, which let her know he was taking off his clothes. She wanted to look up and drink in his sexy male beauty, but didn't dare. Her Dom hadn't given her permission yet.

He kicked off his cowboy boots. When his jeans landed to the side of her, the temptation to take a peek was too great. She slowly and cautiously lifted her gaze.

"Naughty sub," he said with a smile.

"I'm sorry, Sir," she said, but didn't lower her eyes. *God, he is gorgeous, just like I remember.* Lucas stood in front of her in only black boxers. *Nothing has changed in that department.* Even the Wolfe brothers' choices of underwear gave a hint to their distinct personalities. Lucas wore boxers. Jason white briefs. Mitchell always went commando. She grinned, recalling so many other things she loved about the trio.

"Okay, stand up, baby."

"Yes, Sir."

He put his hand on her shoulders. "I need to feel this body, every inch, every curve. I want to be inside you, stretching your pussy with my cock." He grabbed her hands, still locked together by his leather belt, and brought them to his boxers. She could feel his hard, monstrous cock under the fabric. "You want to see it again, don't you, sub?"

She nodded, feeling her lips quiver.

"Take off my underwear," he ordered.

Though it was difficult with the belt on her wrists, she obeyed instantly. When he stepped out of his shorts, he pulled her in close, and she could feel every hot inch of his muscled frame, his erection pressing against her body.

He tilted her head up, capturing her lusty mouth with his, tracing her lips with his hot tongue. She could feel his masculine fingers massaging her breasts again, causing her nipples to become taut. The burn there swirled through her body, settling between her thighs, causing her clit to ache even more.

She was lost to him. He was right that she was his.

Heaven help me, I always have been his. Mitchell's and Jason's, too.

No matter how hard she tried to push them away, the Wolfe brothers inhabited every second of her thoughts. Breakup or not, she belonged to them.

Her heart beat faster and faster as Lucas deepened his kiss and moved one of his hands down her sides, sending his fingers between her legs to the inside of her thighs, teasing her into madness. So familiar…so right.

He released her lips and she saw an urgency in his eyes that was unfamiliar. He was on the edge of his control, and so was she.

Three years. God, I need this. I need him.

She shifted her hips to try to get his hand where she so desperately needed it—on her pussy.

He moved his hand a fraction of an inch from her clit.

"Please," she begged, needing his touch, angling her body again.

He laughed, keeping his fingers just out of reach. "Who is in charge here?"

"You are, Sir."

"Damn right, I am." He threaded his hand through her soaked folds and then circled her clit, increasing the pressure that had been building since their first kiss tonight. "Tell me what you want, sub."

"Please, Lucas. Please." The words spilled out of her like a tsunami. Her emotions were set free now, brought on by his dominance. She'd kept them in check for years, but now that they were out and running, she could not hold back. "I want you inside me, Sir. I need to feel you again. It's been so long."

"You are so beautiful." He removed the belt from her wrists. Gone were the slow tactics she'd remembered. "Damn right it's been too long." He was also in a rush, and she loved every lusty, hurried second. *I need him.*

He placed his hand under her arms, lifting her up. She wrapped her arms around his neck. He lowered her down onto his cock, keeping hold of her. She could feel the head of his cock hit her clit, igniting every nerve inside her. He thrust his dick into her pussy, deep into her, stretching and claiming every inch of her most intimate flesh, causing her to gasp.

I'm his. He's my Dom.

His strokes slammed into her, sending her over the edge.

Sensations, electric and hot, shook her to her core. "Yes. My Dom. Yes."

She watched his eyes narrow as he thrust into her one final time. Her pussy clenched and unclenched, again and again, as she could feel him come inside her. *This feels so right. I've missed this. I've missed him.*

Lucas enveloped her with his muscular arms. She stared at him and saw everything she had always loved about Lucas in his dark brown eyes.

He crashed his sensuous mouth to hers, sending his tongue past her lips. Slowly, his kiss softened, gently reminding her how much he loved her.

God help me, I love him, too.

Chapter Four

Lucas saw the morning sun coming in through Phoebe's bedroom, illuminating her beautiful face. After more lovemaking, they'd moved from the living room to her bed late last night.

She'd fallen asleep in his arms, and he'd remained awake for a little while, relishing being with her again. Now, that he held her, he wasn't about to ever let her go.

Stirring in his arms, her blue eyes opened.

"Good morning, baby." He kissed her sweet lips gently. "Would you like me to make us some coffee?"

"In a little while," she said. "I've got to get up and get dressed soon. Jennifer Steele is coming to my office this morning to meet with me. I just want to lay here beside you for a little bit longer."

"That sounds good to me." He pulled her closer into his body, enjoying the feel of her naked skin against him. *This is where you belong, in my arms.* "I love you, Phoebe Blue."

"I love you, too, but—"

"No 'buts,' sweetheart. Not now. Not ever."

Her eyes widened suddenly. "Oh my God."

"What's wrong?" he asked, realizing she was tensing up.

"We didn't use protection last night." She brought her hands up to her mouth. "What if I'm pregnant?"

"Then you just made me the happiest man in the world."

She shook her head. "I've always wanted a baby, but with all three of you."

Growing up in Destiny, he knew what she meant by that. "That's what I want, too." Paternity testing never occurred. Like his two dads, fathers in poly families cared not about biology. The children belonged to all of them equally.

"We're moving too fast."

"Fast? It's been three years. I would call that slow."

She fixed him with that devilish gaze he'd always loved. "So what happened with you just spending the night and sleeping on the couch? That just didn't work out for you, did it?" Her lips turned up into a teasing smile.

"I think it worked out just right for both of us. We are back together, where we belong."

She clasped her fingers together, as she'd always done whenever she was wrestling with some issue. "You and I might've worked through things last night, but I am still not sure what is going to happen between your brothers and me."

He already had plans for his brothers. "Honey, it's always been their hearts' desire for us to be together again."

"They aren't you, Lucas." She looked down at her hands. "You and I both know that I saw Mitchell with Kaylyn last night. He looked so happy beside her, and I'm really not sure about Jason. I'm not even sure about myself."

She'd always worried too much. "Phoebe, you need to take one step at a time. Trust me. We can get back to how it was. I see that now."

"But if I'm pregnant, I don't have time to take one step at a time."

"We've already started with the first step. And I'm going to get the second step started today."

"What is the second step? I have so much on my plate, Lucas. The Steele case. This stalker issue. Helping Shane."

He stroked her hair. "You have always been the overachiever, baby. That's just one of the many things I love about you. I'm going to help you with everything. Until the stalker is found, me, Mitchell, or Jason will be at your side."

"But—"

"No 'buts.'" He put his finger to her lips. "Hear me out. I'm calling Mitchell now." He knew she wasn't ready to face Jason just yet. As soon as possible, he would go see Jason and fill him in on everything. "You two need time alone. You have your meeting with Jennifer and I've got to go to the Stone Ranch to show Amber some changes to the dormitory plans this morning. Mitchell can be your bodyguard today while I'm gone, and that'll give you time to talk to him about everything."

"I hope you're right about all of this, Lucas. I'm still getting used to us being back together again. I'm still not sure how it's going to turn out with Mitchell and Jason."

"You know, under the circumstances, that time is of the essence. We all want the same thing. So let's move on it."

"I know you're right, but I'm just scared. It's been so long. Are you sure everything is going to turn out okay?"

He kissed her. "Trust me."

"Okay," she said, leaning into him. "Promise me my heart won't be broken again."

"Believe me, baby. My brothers still love you just as much as I do. Leave everything to me." Lucas knew getting Jason and Phoebe to open up to each other was going to be difficult, but not impossible because the love was still there inside them. But they were both very stubborn. Lucas kissed her on the forehead. "You go get ready for your meeting and I will call Mitchell."

She smiled. "Yes, Sir."

Watching her trot off to the bathroom, he'd never been happier that they were together again. But his mind slammed back to the call from the stalker he'd received last night. He clenched his jaw. The woman of his dreams required protection and there were only two men he would trust with that task. The plan was to go to Mitchell first and then Jason.

He retrieved his cell from the nightstand. "Time for step two."

* * * *

Mitchell hit the snare, ending the last song. He'd finally found the sound that he'd been seeking for years. Adding Kaylyn's voice to the mix created what he'd heard in his head that night he'd been holding Phoebe under the stars at Lover's Beach.

"Mitchell, I'm beat," Big Jim said. "I've got to get some shut-eye."

"Just a couple more. Please." He and the band had jammed all night and into the morning after the O'Learys' party with Kaylyn.

Hank turned to their new lead singer. "I told you he never tires."

"I don't think he needs sleep," Big Jim added with a laugh.

Godric yawned. "I could go for another thirty minutes."

Kaylyn stepped away from the keyboard. "I'm toast. I've had fun, Mitchell, but I've got to run. My dogs need to be fed and I'm supposed to be at the sheriff's office."

"I'm sorry for keeping you so long. I forgot you were filling in for Jason until he can find a replacement for Shannon." Destiny wouldn't be the same without the lovely lady.

Kaylyn frowned. "I still can't believe she's gone."

"None of us can." The sweet woman was a fixture in Destiny. "Go," he told them. "Can you all be back tonight at seven?"

"I can't," Kaylyn said. "I've got some more training with Jaris and Sugar, his new guide dog."

Hank asked, "Jaris was Nicole's former partner at the Chicago PD, right?"

She nodded.

Big Jim placed his guitar in its case. "Is Chance working with him, too?"

Everyone in town knew that Kaylyn had a big crush on the guy.

"Yes. He'll be there, too."

Mitchell admired her dedication to the blind. She'd provided some of the best guide dogs to people around the world. Would she be able to let that life go when their big break came? "How about tomorrow night? We're supposed to play at Jena's wedding. Are you ready for that?"

"Sure." She picked up her purse from the counter where she'd left it.

He couldn't believe his luck. Finding Kaylyn was going to change everything. "Kaylyn, you were amazing. Thank you."

"I had fun." She yawned as she dug through her purse. "I'll bring my own keyboard with me tomorrow."

"You will be going to Denver with us, right?" Hank asked her. "We need you for that gig."

"Sure, fellas. I love singing, but you have to know that raising my dogs is my passion. That will always be first."

Mitchell's gut tightened. Now that he'd found the sound, would he be able to keep it if Kaylyn had other dreams?

"I'm happy being second if you sing with us from time to time." Godric grinned. The guy fit in perfectly with all of them, and he was a great bass player, too. "You're so talented, Kaylyn."

Big Jim nodded. "She's got the best pipes I've ever heard."

After saying their good-byes, the band exited Mitchell's garage just as his cell went off.

Who would be calling him this early? *Everyone in town knows I played last night at the party.* He looked at the name on his screen. *Lucas.*

"Why are you calling me this time of day?" he asked. "You know I don't get up before ten after a gig."

"Phoebe's in trouble."

His jaw clenched. She was his muse—always. Even after the breakup, he still pictured only her face during every song he played. She was the inspiration for the sound he'd finally found last night. "What kind of trouble is she in?"

"Her stalker is back. She needs us, Mitchell."

"Where is she?"

"With me. I'm at her house."

That was all he needed to hear. "I'll be there in two minutes."

"Perfect." Lucas paused. "We're going to get her back, Mitchell."

He heard something odd in his brother's voice that shocked him. He'd seen them on the sofa during Patrick's speech. Had they spent the night together?

This was no time to let false hope derail him. Phoebe needed him. She was in trouble. That was all that mattered now. "You can fill me in on the rest when I get there."

* * * *

Jason looked at the time on his cell and realized Shane was already five minutes late for their meeting.

Fuck. Same old Shane.

Kaylyn walked into his office. "Would you like some coffee, Sheriff?" She yawned.

"I think you're the one who needs coffee. How late did you stay at the O'Learys'?"

"It wasn't the O'Learys'. I spent the whole night with Mitchell...I mean...your brother...and the band."

"You what?" Mitchell and Kaylyn?

"I mean...I'm making this worse." She shook her head. "Let's start again."

"That would be the place to begin," he said with a grin.

"Mitchell found out that I was a singer last night at the party. So, we all went to his house and we practiced all night. I guess you know that Nancy is leaving. Wolfe Mayhem has a gig in Denver. They need me to be ready. So, of course, I spent the night with them."

"So you said." Kaylyn was fun to tease.

She put her hands on her hips. "Stop it, Jason. We jammed all night. That's all." She smiled. "I was rambling, wasn't I?"

"You were, but that's okay. Why don't you head home and get

some sleep. I can handle things here just fine. By the way, I didn't know you were a singer."

"Mostly in the shower, but yes I can sing. Anyway, I promised you I would help and that's what I will do. I can sleep tonight."

"Anyone here?" a voice he recognized came from the exterior office.

"We're in here, Shane," Kaylyn said.

Phoebe's brother walked in, cocky as usual. "Kaylyn, you look beautiful as always."

"And you're letting your hair grow out. I like it."

"You can thank the better barbers outside of the prison system for that."

"You're late, Blue," Jason snapped.

Shane shrugged. "You're the one who changed the time, so I had to rearrange my schedule to accommodate you, Wolfe."

"You will address me as Sheriff Wolfe. Don't forget I am your parole officer."

"How can I forget with you constantly reminding me of that fact?"

"Fellas, I'm going to make a new pot of coffee," Kaylyn said. "I think we all woke up on the wrong side of the bed this morning. I'll make it good and strong." She rushed out the door.

"Sit down, Blue," he said, refusing to call him by his given name. Shane had hurt Phoebe. Case closed. Besides, Shane hadn't called him by name since returning to Destiny either. They may have been friends before Shane's fuck up, but never again.

The felon smirked and took his time taking a seat. "Let's get this over with, Wolfe. I have places to be and people to see."

"Right now, the only place you need to be is in my office and the only person you need to see is me." Anger boiled inside him, recalling the time he and Shane went to blows at the diner.

"Have you gotten a job yet?"

"I've only been out a few weeks, so no. I haven't." Shane put his hands behind his head. "Tick-tock, Sheriff. Next?"

What happened to the old Shane, the guy he loved as much as his own brothers? He was gone. He never could understand the sudden change in Phoebe's brother. No one could. It just didn't make sense.

Jason pointed to the book on his desk that he'd gotten out for this meeting. "These are the Colorado statutes that govern how a parolee and their supervising officer conduct the process."

He grinned. "God, you're not going to read that thing to me are you, Jason?"

"I will if I want to," he said, shocked that Shane had called him by name. *Clearly, a slipup.* Maybe there was a chance to help Phoebe's brother after all, but he didn't hold much hope for him. The odds for a felon who had committed a crime like Shane's to become a repeat offender were very high. Jason closed the book and opened Shane's folder. "You've had two drug tests."

"Clean as a whistle. Doc Ryder told me so."

"So far, Blue. So far."

Kaylyn came in with two cups of coffee, with Dylan following behind.

"Everything okay?" He wondered if Dylan had found out any more about Mitrofanov's whereabouts or the five million dollars of the Knight's money still missing.

"I just need a minute with my cousin, Sheriff, if you don't mind."

"Why not? We're done here today." He wondered what Dylan had to say to Shane. Probably just some family business. Shane's mother, Alice, was sister to Jane, Dylan's mother. Of all the men who had been brought up in the Blue and Strange households, only Shane had fallen on the wrong side of life. Corey was a US marshal. Dylan an agent of the CIA, and his brother Cameron was CFO at TBK and honest as the day was long. Why Shane had turned out the way he had just didn't make any sense.

"Here you go, fellows." Kaylyn handed him the cup. "Black for the sheriff. Cream and sugar for you, Shane."

"You remembered," Blue said, taking his. "Thank you."

"Dylan, would you like a cup?" Kaylyn asked.

He shook his head. "No thank you."

The phone at the desk in the other office rang. "Back on the job," she said, leaving them.

"Blue, I'll see you in a week. You better have a job by then. Am I clear?"

"Crystal."

"Then you can go. Dylan, I'd like to talk to you about that other matter when you're finished with your cousin, if you don't mind."

Kaylyn returned, her face white. "It's for you and Dylan, Sheriff. A woman named Brown."

"Put her through." She probably wanted to update him on the case.

Kaylyn shook her head. "She already hung up. She's coming over now."

"What else did she say, Kaylyn?" Dylan asked.

"Kip Lunceford has escaped."

Chapter Five

Phoebe came out of her bathroom, expecting to see Lucas, but found Mitchell standing in her hallway instead. "Where's Lucas?"

"Gone." Mitchell had made her heart melt with his songs. She'd missed their private jam sessions for far too long. "He'll be back tomorrow morning. He's going to stay up at the Stone Ranch tonight. They're working around the clock to get the dorm done by the deadline. I'm your new bodyguard for now."

"He told you about the calls from the stalker?"

"Yes, he did. But he also told me there's a lot more you want to talk about."

"There is," she said, recalling seeing Mitchell talking to Kaylyn last night. "But I'm in a rush." She looked at the time on her phone. "Jennifer Steele is going to be at my office in five minutes for our meeting. I don't want to be late."

"Then let's go. But we will talk later, understand?"

Mitchell wasn't going to let her off the hook, and she was glad about that.

She picked up her briefcase and headed toward the front door. "Yes, we will. I'll tell you everything. It's long overdue."

His eyebrows shot up. "I like the sound of that."

"Perhaps you should hold judgment until after we talk. You know how I can be, Mitchell."

"I love everything about how you can be, Phoebe Blue."

She hoped he would feel the same way once they sat down and hashed things out. Had she waited too long? Was he already in love with Kaylyn?

Taking the keys from her hand, Mitchell locked the door behind them and they walked the short distance to her office.

Ashley was sitting at her desk when Phoebe and Mitchell walked in. "Good morning, boss. Coffee is ready. Everything is set up in the conference room for you. Mrs. Steele is already there." Ashley handed Phoebe a new cell. "I got you a burner phone this time."

"How?" Phoebe wouldn't have the slightest idea where to get one.

"Jena Taylor suggested I do that instead of a regular phone."

"Jena would know how to avoid contact after all her years of running from her ex," Mitchell said.

"She's not running any longer." Ashley had become close to Jena over the past month. "Don't forget her wedding is Saturday night at the chapel, boss. Seven sharp."

"I won't. Mom is catering the reception."

"Boss, don't give this number to anyone other than me and your family." Ashley turned to Mitchell and smiled. "And men that you trust. No one else."

"Got it." Recalling the call from the stalker, Phoebe turned to Mitchell.

He grabbed her hands. "I'm not going anywhere, honey. I'll wait out here until you're done."

Same Mitchell she'd always known. He could always read her mind.

"Thank you."

He sent her a loving wink and then looked at Ashley. "How about some of that coffee? I could really use some."

Ashley grinned. "Looks like you had a long night."

"Don't go there, Ash. Cart before the horse, if you know what I mean."

"I always do know what you mean, boss. I also know what's good for you. That's why you pay me so well. You better get in there, Phoebe. I'll take care of your man."

"My man?" Phoebe smiled, loving the sound of those two words together. "I should dock your pay right now for insubordination."

"Don't you dare," Mitchell jumped in. "She deserves a raise in my opinion."

"Didn't ask for your opinion, Mr. Wolfe," she teased.

Ashley laughed. "Don't listen to her, Mitchell. She knows I'm right. I have some cinnamon rolls I picked up from Blue's earlier, too. How does that sound?"

"Perfect," he said, taking a seat on the sofa. "I'm starving."

Phoebe walked into the conference room, praying Ashley was right. "Hi, Jennifer."

"Hello, counselor," her client and friend answered.

Phoebe needed to get her head back to this case. Jennifer deserved her best. She was a strong woman. Losing Bill twelve years ago had crushed her, but she'd survived, taking charge of the vast ranching Steele Empire.

"How's my case?"

"With the files I got from your vet showing your cattle had a clean bill of health, I believe we can get Braxton to drop this suit." Phoebe took a seat. "I've interviewed several people involved in the sale and transportation of your cattle to their processing plant. I've got one thing left on my list. Ashley and I are going to Chicago next week to talk to their staff vet, the man who said your cattle tested positive for mad cow. I'm sure there's been a mix-up. Once I see his files, this might be over then."

Jennifer listened to every detail that she'd uncovered.

When Phoebe finished, the reigning unattached queen of the subs of Phase Four grabbed her hand. "Thank you, Phoebe. I don't know what I would have done without you."

"The same for me, Jen. May I talk to you about something?"

"Of course."

"It's about the Wolfe brothers."

"I knew something was up when I saw you at the Halloween party holding Lucas's hand." Jennifer smiled. "Talk to me."

"I'm about to go down the rabbit hole with the Wolfe brothers again. Hopefully, it's going to be good for me like Ashley believes, but I'm afraid I'll get my heart broken again."

"Honey, for years I've watched and seen how they look at you at every event we have. I've also seen how you look at them. It's evident that you are still in love with each other. So, I say it's past time you got this situation straightened out for the good of all four of you."

"But what about Shane and all that happened between him and Jason? How can we get past that?" She wanted to so badly. She loved her men.

"You've never tried, have you? If I remember correctly, you closed them out. In all my years, I've always discovered that if you try, you can find a solution. Bill and I had a wonderful marriage, but we, too, had our bumps in the road."

"Everyone does, I suppose." Bill had died when Jen was only twenty-nine. Now, twelve years later, Phoebe could see she was stronger than most, though her heart was clearly still broken.

Jen nodded. "The only way we got through them was to be honest with each other, truly honest. God, I miss that man."

Phoebe grabbed her hand. "We all do, Jen."

The woman's eyes brimmed with tears. "Sweetie, love is worth the risk. Trust me."

* * * *

Mitchell opened the entrance door of Phong's Wok for Phoebe. They walked inside.

"Two?" Hiro Phong, the owner asked.

"Yes," he told him. "Can we have a booth away from the window?"

"You betcha," the man answered. Hiro's English was perfect, thanks to his wife of three decades, Melissa, who was from Missouri. He handed them menus as they sat down.

Mitchell made sure he had his back to the wall so he could get the best view of the entire restaurant, including the entrance and the windows. Phoebe sat across from him. He wasn't about to take any chances with her safety.

Hiro smiled. "I'll bring you some hot tea. Phoebe, right?"

"Yes. Thank you."

"Water for you, Mitchell?"

"Usually, but today, may I have coffee instead?"

"You got it, cowboy." Hiro rushed back to the kitchen as more Destonians filed into the restaurant.

"I'm starving," Phoebe said with a grin, which thrilled him. "Mitchell Wolfe, you didn't leave me one cinnamon roll. You still have that big appetite I remember."

"You're right, and that's why I'm hungry again." It felt good to be so relaxed around her. Really good. "I'm going to start with egg rolls and crab puffs, followed by sesame chicken with fried rice."

"Are you sure that's enough?" she teased.

He smiled. "Actually, I'll have dessert after."

Joshua, Phong's son and the Knight's pilot, walked in with a person Mitchell didn't recognize. The guy resembled Josh some, though from his mother's side only.

Hiro stepped up to the duo, handing them aprons. "I need your help today. Dishwasher and hostess both called in sick."

"It's my lunch hour," Joshua protested.

"Uncle Hiro, I've never waited tables before," the other man said.

"Jacob, no time like the present. Josh, I only need you for the rush. Help an old man out, boys."

"You got it, Pop." Josh winked. "I'll help you, Jacob."

"Looks like we might have to wait on your food for a while, Mitchell." Phoebe grabbed his hand and gave him one of her mocking looks. God, he'd missed her. "I hope you will survive, Mr. Wolfe."

"How much time do you normally take for lunch, counselor?"

"An hour, but Ashley's got everything covered. I need to pick up my dress for Jena's wedding Saturday and then I plan on working from home this afternoon. No court dates today."

"Works for me."

"Besides, I think my bodyguard needs to stretch out on my sofa and get some much-needed rest. When was the last time you slept?"

He shrugged. "Night before last, but that doesn't matter. I'm here for you."

"I know, and you can't imagine how much that means to me. But when we get to my house, I'm determined you get to take a nap."

God, he loved her fire. He missed being with her.

Joshua walked over and handed them their drinks. "Nice to see you two together."

"It's only lunch, Josh." Phoebe grinned. "Don't jump to conclusions."

"I'm not the only one who is assuming that you two might be back together." Joshua motioned to several customers who were glancing their direction. "You know how the people in Destiny are, Phoebe."

She nodded and smiled.

Everyone seemed acutely interested in her and Mitchell, even Belle White, Amber's sister, who wasn't even a native of the town.

"Just take our order, please."

Phoebe ordered sweet and sour chicken.

Feeling his stomach roll, he added another entrée to the list. "And more coffee, please."

"I'll have mom put on a new pot. Thanks." Josh walked away.

Mitchell looked over at Phoebe, who was the most beautiful woman he'd ever seen. "Lucas told me that you wanted to talk."

She nodded. "I do, but let's have our lunch first. Okay?"

"I've waited three years to talk, honey. If all I have to do is wait a few more minutes, that will be just fine with me."

"Thank you. I just need to get my thoughts clear before we dive in. Besides, you're starving, right?"

He reached across the table and grabbed her hands. He could feel her tremble. "I've been starving to be with you again, Phoebe. Whatever time you need, I'll give it to you. I can see it in your eyes. You're ready to give us another shot, aren't you?"

Phoebe looked down at their joined hands. "Maybe, but there's so much to discuss before we go there, Mitchell."

"Then we'll discuss it." It was the most important thing in the world to him. He wouldn't mess up this chance.

"After we eat, okay?"

"Deal."

Jacob and Josh brought over their lunch, which covered the entire table.

He and Phoebe ate the delicious food and sat quietly together.

I love this woman. God, how I love her.

When the door to the restaurant opened again, still on alert, Mitchell glanced that direction. Phoebe's two brothers walked in. Seeing Shane made him tense. His old friend's fuck up had been the catalyst to fuel the breakup.

Both Phoebe's brothers were staring at Belle. It was obvious they were attracted to her, but he couldn't imagine any way that the two of them could share her or any other woman for that matter, given their opposite backgrounds.

"Your brothers are here," he told Phoebe, since her back was to the door.

Her eyes widened. "Maybe they're here for lunch like we are." She turned around.

"Sis," Shane said, heading their direction.

Corey followed.

Mitchell saw the looks on her brothers' faces. "Apparently it's more than lunch for them, honey."

"Scoot," Shane told her.

"Sure." She slid over, making room for him in the booth next to her. "Are you here to eat? Our food was delicious, as usual."

"We're not here for lunch, Phoebe." Corey took a seat next to

Mitchell. "We're here to talk about your stalker."

"Damn right, we are," Shane said firmly. "Why haven't you told us about this, sis?"

"Shane, you have too much on your plate for me to bother you with something that might not even be a big deal."

"Someone stalking my little sister is a very big deal."

"Damn right, it is," Corey agreed.

"Did Lucas call you?" Phoebe's feistiness was back in full. She wasn't going to be steamrolled by anyone, even her brothers. "Or Ashley?"

"Lucas told us," Corey answered.

Shane frowned. "Ashley is going to get a piece of my mind later for not letting us know."

"Leave Ashley alone," Phoebe shot back. "I made her promise. She answers to me."

Corey tapped his fingers on the table. "How long has this been going on, Phoebe?"

Phoebe gave them all the details, which was even more than Mitchell had heard.

"I'm going to get this fucker." Shane's face was blood red. "I'm going to put a bullet between his eyes."

Even though he wasn't sure he could ever trust Shane again, he actually was in agreement with his idea. Anyone who wanted to hurt Phoebe didn't deserve to live.

"Since you are not allowed to carry a gun while you're on parole, brother, I doubt you can do that." Phoebe's tone was steady but Mitchell could sense the storm of worry brewing under her calm demeanor. She cared deeply for both her brothers but felt responsible for Shane. "This is exactly why I didn't want to tell the family about this. I absolutely don't want Mom and Dads to know. Do you both understand me?"

"I agree." Shane's face took on a shadow of guilt.

In that moment, Mitchell saw a glimpse of the old Shane he

remembered.

Belle walked over to their table with Juan. "Sorry to interrupt, but I need to talk to Shane."

Shane's eyes lit up at the blonde beauty's words. "You do?"

"Amber and I want to offer you a job at the Boys Ranch. Lucas told us this morning that you were looking. Is that right?"

Shane shrugged. "The sheriff says I should be."

"Shane, we could really use your help." Belle put her arm around Juan. "We're on a tight time schedule to get the dorm ready before the rest of the boys show up. We're housing the five early arrivals at Amber's place. Twelve more will be showing up in December. We just don't have much time."

Corey and Phoebe were watching Shane, clearly hoping he would take the job. Their belief in their brother was something to behold. Mitchell wished for a turnaround in Shane, but he just wasn't sure it would happen.

"Belle, helping you would be a fun job to me." Shane winked and Belle smiled. "Would you like me to start now?"

"Mr. Shane, I'll show you the baby horse that Lady Dancer gave birth to this morning." Juan grinned. "Uncle Emmett said he's mine. I'm calling him Dragon Seeker."

"Good name, Juan." Mitchell smiled, happy to have another believer in town.

"Why don't you have Corey bring you around five and we'll have dinner?" Belle asked. "That way I can show you both around."

Clearly, the woman was just as attracted to Phoebe's brothers as they were to her. Belle might have only been in Destiny for a short time, but she was getting acclimated really fast.

Corey smiled. "I'll be glad to bring him to the ranch, Belle,"

"Yes." Juan's excitement was evident to all of them. "Mr. Corey, I'll show you Dragon Seeker, too."

The marshal put his hand on Juan's shoulder. "Looking forward to it."

Belle smiled. "Gentlemen, I'll see you tonight." She turned to Phoebe and Mitchell. "Sorry to interrupt your lunch."

Shane's face lit up like a beacon. "It was our pleasure, Belle."

Juan and Belle headed out the door.

Mitchell's cell rang. "This might be Lucas."

Phoebe sighed. "I bet he's contacted Jason about the latest calls I got from my stalker. Apparently the whole town needs to know about this."

"Of course he has," Corey said flatly. "Jason is still the sheriff, sis. He should know everything when it happens."

"Hello," Mitchell said into his phone.

"Another brother with my woman?" a computerized-sounding voice asked. "You Wolfes will pay. She's mine."

What the hell? "Look, you motherfucker—"

His cell went dead.

Chapter Six

"Mitchell?" Phoebe's heart thudded in her chest, anxiety flooding her entire body. "Was that...*him*?"

He nodded, and she stopped breathing.

"Fuck. I wonder how the bastard is able to get your numbers." Shane's tone was full of rage.

This was exactly why she hadn't told her family about the calls. The last thing Shane and the rest of the Blues needed was to worry about her problem.

"And how does he know you were with our sister?" Corey asked Mitchell, assuming his typical big-brother role. "Does he know who you are?"

"No clue. We need to be on the lookout for a stranger in town," Mitchell's overprotective nature was in high gear, and she had to admit she was happy about that. "If anyone sees any outsiders, they need to report to Jason."

"In the meantime, she's not to be alone," Corey demanded. "We can all take different shifts."

"No." Mitchell shook his head. "My brothers and I have this under control."

Shane's eyebrows shot up. "Jason, too? I doubt that. Even if that's true, she is *our sister.*"

"And she is my responsibility, like it or not," he stated firmly, grabbing her hand.

Corey stood. "I want to talk to Jason and see how he plans on finding your stalker. Phoebe, you're with me."

Mitchell's face darkened. "I thought I made myself clear, Corey."

This was getting out of hand. "That's enough. I love how protective you are all being with me, but I'm a grown woman." She turned to Corey and Shane. "Thanks, but I'm going to stay with Mitchell. Besides, since Corey and Jason are both lawmen, the two of you can hammer out what needs to be done better without me. Right now, I need to talk to Mitchell alone. It's very important to me."

Shane nodded and put his arm around her shoulders. "Sis, I do trust Mitchell."

She looked in his eyes and saw a hint of regret. "So do I."

Shane turned to his old friend. "You'll keep her safe?"

Mitchell nodded. "With my very life, Shane."

"You better come with me then, brother," Corey said.

"Why not?" Shane stood. "Jason and I haven't seen enough of each other today."

Corey bent down and kissed her on the cheek. "No more keeping me in the dark, sis."

"I won't."

Shane looked at Mitchell and her. "Call if you hear or see or learn anything else about the bastard."

"We will," Mitchell replied.

She looked at Shane, praying he would follow all the requirements of his parole. The last thing she wanted was for her stalker situation to somehow derail her brother. "I promise."

Corey walked over to Hiro. "If you see any strangers here, I want to be called immediately, Mr. Phong."

"Trouble?"

"It's Destiny," Shane said. "There's always trouble brewing here."

"I will call you, Marshal. Haven't seen anyone lately. Not since the Russian's house exploded anyway."

Corey and Shane turned back her direction for a moment, then they left.

She loved her overprotective brothers, especially now.

Mitchell put his arm around her shoulders. "Time to go home, baby."

"Lead the way, Mr. Wolfe."

* * * *

Mitchell sat next to Phoebe on her sofa. She'd poured them both a glass of wine. It was evident to him that she was having trouble getting out what was on her mind, so he decided to take the bull by the horns and dive in. "I'll go first."

She nodded. "I'd like that very much."

"When Lucas called me this morning about him being with you, he told me that he had explained everything to you. Do you understand why we turned Shane over to Jason back then?" He held his breath as he waited for her answer.

"You thought it was the right thing to do." Her voice was barely a whisper. "I get that now."

"Phoebe, what happened to Shane broke my heart. I've always loved him like my own brother. But when Lucas and I found the marijuana in his sleeping bag, we honestly did not know what to do. We'd never experienced anything like it before. We felt we could fix this before you had to know about it, not realizing the whole thing was going to blow up sky high. Our whole plan, our whole intention, was just to get him help. It turned out all wrong." If he could go back in time and change the way he handled it, he would. Unfortunately, life didn't work that way.

"I know, Mitchell. You all meant well."

"Lucas and I only went to Jason because we knew he would know what steps to take to get Shane into rehab. Had we thought Jason was going to throw the book at him, we wouldn't have. I swear." He still didn't understand Jason's actions.

Tears rolled down Phoebe's cheeks. "It was such an emotional time. I let my mind convince me that you never really cared for me. If you did, I thought, how could you hurt my brother that way? Hurt me that way?"

"I'm sorry we handled it all wrong. I hate that I hurt you." She had to accept his apology. His whole world depended on it.

"We all did things we regret," she said softly. "I was so convinced I closed the door on all of you. When Shane came back from prison, my heart started to change. I realized I let the three men I loved most in the world walk right out of my life. For three years, I kept telling myself I was doing the right thing. But every time I saw any of you, my heart broke a little more."

"I believe all of our hearts were broken, sweetheart." He reached out and touched her hand. "It's been far too long."

Her delicate fingers curled around his, filling him with such joy.

He leaned forward and kissed her tenderly.

She returned the kiss but suddenly pushed him back.

"What's wrong?" Was it too soon?

"I'm not here to break up you and Kaylyn."

What was she talking about? "Kaylyn? Kaylyn Anderson?"

"Yes. Mitchell, I saw you two together last night at the O'Learys' Halloween party. And the closeness between the two of you was obvious." She leaned back, folding her arms over her chest, reminding him of how stubborn she could be.

He laughed, realizing what Phoebe had seen at the party. "You've mixed things up in your pretty little head."

"I know what I saw. This is a mistake. You have every right to move on. Three years. I can't expect you not to go on with your life. That's not fair."

He couldn't move on with his life without her. "It's the sound, baby."

She shook her head. "What? Sound? How tired are you? Maybe we should talk about this later."

"Honey, remember that night you and I made love under the stars."

She smiled. "I'll never forget. It was our first time together."

"You fell asleep in my arms. God, that was a great night."

"It was, Mitchell, but I still don't understand what that has to do with Kaylyn."

He grabbed her hands. "That night I told you about the sound I heard in my mind. Remember?"

She nodded.

"You, lovely lady, are the music. You always have been my muse." Overwhelmed by his love for her, he pulled her in close and squeezed her tightly. "Though some know I've been seeking out our sound, you alone know how long I've been searching."

"I do," she said sweetly. "Since Lover's Beach."

"Last night, I heard Kaylyn singing and I knew I'd found it, Phoebe. I found *our* sound—our music." Again, there were no words to express what he was feeling for her. *Only the music—our music.* "You have to hear it. The band practiced all night with Kaylyn. It's amazing."

"Oh my God, Mitchell. I had no idea Kaylyn could sing. I'm so happy for you."

"For me? For us. For you and me." He devoured her mouth, recalling their first time on the blanket under the stars. He felt her lips part, welcoming his kiss. He sent his tongue into her moist mouth, hearing the music fire up in his head again after long last. "I love you, Phoebe. I've never stopped loving you. I will always love you."

"I love you, too. No matter how much I tried to push you out of my heart, it always belonged to you."

He lifted her off the sofa and into his arms. "You're mine, baby."

She leaned her head into his chest. "Yes, Sir. I'm yours."

Hearing her submissive tone caused his cock to harden and his balls to grow heavy. He carried her into the bedroom, gently placing her on her comforter. "It's been far too long, sweetheart."

He bent down and unbuttoned her blouse and she reached up and unbuttoned his shirt. Removing her silky bra, he skimmed his hands over her perfect breasts. "God, you feel so good."

The way she moved her fingertips over his chest deepened his connection to her. They were rediscovering each other's body, becoming enmeshed again in the love they'd buried.

"I love you so much, Phoebe. God, I was a fool to let you walk away. I swear I will never let you go."

"I won't ever walk away again, Mitchell. I love you so much. I trust you with my heart."

Her words thrilled him beyond belief. Her love and trust were all he'd ever wanted.

Mad for the taste of her lips, he kissed her again. "You're mine."

"I'm yours."

Another possessive kiss. "My baby."

"My man."

He kissed her neck, enjoying the softness of her skin. "I've missed you so much."

She kissed him back. "I'll never go away again. I promise. I need you, Mitchell. I need you so much."

Lost to the intense, familiar emotions, they undressed each other slowly, kissing and caressing and touching. It was as if they couldn't get enough of each other.

He'd never felt like this with any other woman, so in sync, so connected, so right.

* * * *

Phoebe looked into Mitchell's eyes and felt her desire for him explode.

He kissed her taut nipples, adding to her hot shivers. *Why? Why did I starve myself of this amazing man?* Three years without him had left her empty and lost.

She grabbed hold of his cock, her need so great, so demanding. Unable to bring her fingers together around his girth, she remembered how wonderful it was to touch him, to feel him, to surrender her body to his.

I'm with him again.

"I love you with all my heart," Mitchell said. He had always expressed his emotions for her without hesitation from the very beginning. She loved hearing every word.

"I love you, too."

He moved down her abdomen, kissing her tenderly, creating a line to the place she needed him most. When his mouth covered her pussy, she gasped, memories of their past times together flooding through every thought, every cell, everywhere.

Wrapping her legs around his neck, she grabbed the back of his head, lost to her desire for him to claim her once again. Her need for him to go deeper was more than she could bear. "Please, Mitchell. God, I need you. I've needed you for such a very long time."

"You have me, Phoebe. I'm yours. Now and forever." His hot tongue hit her clit and created an explosion inside her body.

Unable to hold herself back, she came. Sensations shot through her, hot and electric. Every inch of her seemed to ignite, as she thrashed under him. "Yes. Yes. Yes."

"Give me your cream, baby. Every drop." He licked her into a frenzied state.

She could barely catch her breath. "I need you deep inside me, Mitchell."

"I want that, too, baby." He moved his body until the tip of his cock was pressing on her swollen folds. "I love you with all my heart." He thrust his dick deep inside her pussy, filling her so completely.

"I love you, Mitchell. God, how I love you."

Her words seemed to spur him on more as he sent his cock in and out of her pussy, adding to her pleasure.

Deeper and deeper he went. His thrusts came faster. On and on. The intensity was so powerful, as if they were both trying to make up for the past they'd lost.

Over and over.

They both were so close, the pressure building and multiplying. Together, they came, lost to the incredible release they'd created together.

"Baby, I hear it. I hear our sound." Mitchell kissed her. "I love you."

"I love you, too."

Overcome with emotions, keeping silent was impossible for both of them. They had to confess their love for each other again and again.

He held her close for some time, until her breathing settled down.

"I can't get enough of you, Phoebe. It's been so long."

"Me either," she said, looking into his beautiful eyes.

He kissed her again, making her tingly and woozy.

She could feel his cock pressing against her thigh.

He moved his hands over her body. "You feel so soft and warm." He nibbled on her neck while gently massaging her breast with his fingers.

"Oh, Mitchell, this feels so good. I'm so happy we're together." She touched his face.

He turned to her, and she kissed him, deeply and passionately. She could feel his cock harden once again, letting her know he wanted her as much as she wanted him. With his amazing mouth on her pussy, he'd sent her over the edge into a sea of wonderful sensations. Now, flooded with overwhelming desire for him, she moved down his body, planting sweet kisses on his muscled frame.

"I know what you're up to, baby, and I can't wait." He flipped around until both their heads were between each other's legs. "I want to sample you again. I'm addicted to you, Phoebe. Every bit of you."

She leaned forward and kissed the head of his cock. "I am, too, Mitchell."

She felt his tongue, once again, lapping on her wet pussy. Wrapping her hands around his muscled thighs, she licked up and down his shaft. Coming to the slit at the tip of his dick, her tongue discovered a pearly drop, which she drank down. His licks on her sex enflamed her more. She swallowed his cock, taking it down her throat. Up and down, she bobbed on the man she'd walked away from.

Never again.

Tears of joy flooded her eyes as his licks began to build the pressure inside her.

He circled her clit with his lusty tongue. She could feel his hands moving over her sensitive flesh. He sent a couple of fingers into her pussy, and she groaned, her mouth full of his dick. When his lips captured her clit, she felt a spasm roll through her entire body. She continued sucking on him, enjoying the feel of his cock pulsing inside her mouth. Bathing him with her tongue and lips, she bobbed up and down, swamped with such an immense thirst. They continued making love to each other with their mouths until she thought she could stand no more, and yet their sixty-nine went on and on.

The rumble of release began in her core as his mouth drank from her body. Liquid poured out of her and she clawed at his legs, continuing to suck on his cock until her cheeks hollowed out. Then he thrust his cock deeper past her lips and she tasted his salty seed hit the back of her throat.

As they released each other, she shifted around and placed her head on his shoulder. "You mean everything to me," she confessed, unable to hold back anything from him now.

"You are my world, Phoebe Blue. We will be together forever." He kissed her gently, squeezing her tightly into him. "Now that I have you in my arms again, I will never let you go."

She smiled. "I'm glad you keep saying that, Mitchell, because I love hearing it."

"And I will continue saying it for as long as I live. I lost you once. Never again."

"I'm here. Right here. In your arms."

He kissed her. "Right where you belong."

Feeling completely sated, they relaxed and fell asleep in each other's arms.

Chapter Seven

Jason, deep in paperwork, heard his office door open.

Corey and Shane walked in, seeming anxious and tense. "Something wrong?"

"Yes, there's something wrong," Shane blurted. "Our sister has a stalker. What are you doing about it, Sheriff?"

"Calm down, Shane," Corey said. "Let Jason talk."

"I've been working on this for weeks, guys. I haven't been sitting still on this one. Besides, it's my job to protect the citizens of Destiny." *I care about her, so even if I wasn't sheriff, I would do whatever I could to protect her, no matter what our current status is…*

"Why didn't you tell us?" Corey's tone was full of frustration and concern.

He couldn't blame him. This was about Phoebe. "Because your sister made me swear to keep your family out of it unless something turned up. So far, it's only been calls from the jerk. I don't have any other leads. With Dylan's help, I've put tracers on every new phone she has, but the fucker hangs up before we can get a lock on his location."

Shane placed his hands on the desk and leaned forward. "How in the hell did the bastard get your brothers' numbers when she was with them, Jason?"

His jaw tightened. "What the hell are you talking about? None of us have been with Phoebe since you got sent away. Not Lucas. Not Mitchell. Not me."

"Not true," Shane said with a smile. "Lucas spent the night with her after the last stalker call. Mitchell is at her house right now, making sure she stays safe."

What the hell is going on? Jason knew things between him and Mitchell and Lucas were tense, but that his brothers would keep him in the dark about what was happening with Phoebe angered him. "I don't think it's time to talk about whether or not me and my brothers and your sister are going to get back together."

"I agree. There's a stalker that is harassing my sister. I want to know all the details you've collected on it. I want every fact, every thread, every trail. Anything you've found, give it to me. I can—"

"Hold on, Blue. This is my county. Not yours." He was impressed by Shane's line of thinking. Had Shane not gone bad, he would've made one helluva good lawman. "Yes, she's you're sister, but you're a convicted felon. I don't want you doing a damn thing on this. Leave it to me. Now, you both better fill me in because apparently I'm out of the loop. What's happened that I'm not aware of?"

They told him about the three calls that had come from the stalker, starting last night before the O'Learys' Halloween party.

The first was to Phoebe herself. It had been a couple of weeks since she'd heard from the asshole. She'd been given a new phone. He still had her old phone in his desk drawer.

The second had gone to Lucas, which puzzled and worried him. Was the stalker in Destiny? He'd considered that as a possibility during his investigation, but had dismissed it after one of Dylan's traces indicated the origination point of one of the calls was Idaho.

The third call had gone to Mitchell, right in front of Corey and Shane at Phong's Wok.

"It's very clear to me that whoever this fucker is, he's got incredible computer skills." He recalled what Brown had told him this morning. *Kip Lunceford has escaped.*

"So who tops your lists of suspects, Sheriff?" Corey asked.

He wasn't going to talk about this in front of Shane. "I'm still compiling names of possibles. As you know, Corey, conducting an investigation takes time, but believe me, I'm dotting every *i* and crossing every *t*. There isn't a stone I'm not turning over."

Now that Jason and Nicole were on Brown's new CIA covert team with Dylan, Matt, Sean, and Jena, the release of any information would have to be cleared, even for Corey, though he was a US marshal.

Could Kip be Phoebe's stalker?

Though Jason wasn't sure how, he knew Kip, the brilliant psychopath, just might be. Lunceford was capable of many things. He'd just escaped from the transport that was taking him to the new prison. Phoebe had been dealing with her stalker issue for months now, so it didn't seem to line up that Lunceford could be the culprit.

But Kip had proven, again and again, he could get past whatever security systems the Feds had. Getting access to make a call to Destiny wouldn't be a challenge at all for him. According to Easton Black, the man who'd given his life to protect Destiny, Lunceford's new residence would keep him locked up tighter than a drum. But Kip had fooled them all, avoiding finishing out his life sentence in the highest maximum-security prison in the country.

Shane paced around the room. "What about any guys she might've dated since your breakup?"

Jason's gut tightened, recalling she had gone out with another guy. After first being brought in on this stalker issue, he'd asked her the same question right here in his office. She'd bristled, but had told him everything. "Since you went to prison, she's been on a few dates." She was moving on. *Fuck.* "One of the senior techs at O'Leary Global took her to dinner a few times. Guy's name is Compton. Remember Mac Doss from high school?"

Corey nodded. "Didn't he move to Clover when we were sophomores?"

"I must've been a freshman." Shane frowned. "How long did they see each other?"

"According to your sister, they had dinner twice. Nothing more." He'd been happy to learn that. "The only other guy on the list is Andy

McCrae."

"Andy McCrae?" Shane clearly didn't know him since the guy had arrived in Destiny when he'd been in prison and had transferred out several months before he'd been paroled.

"He was an analyst at TBK for a couple of years. Long gone. Betty Anderson set Phoebe up with him about a year ago. It went nowhere." Jason remembered Andy well. Phoebe deserved better than that guy. *I wish it could be me, but I know it can't.* "Didn't seem like your sister's type to me. McCrae was a pussy, in my opinion. You should've seen the way he dressed and walked around town. I thought the wind would blow him over."

Shane snorted. "Sounds like someone is a bit jealous to me."

Jason had a great poker face about most things. But when it came to Phoebe, he was as transparent as glass. The whole town knew he still cared about her. "You would've thought the same thing if you'd seen him, Blue."

Shane turned to his brother. "I guess I've been away longer than I realized, Corey."

"What do you mean?"

"I was brought up in Destiny. Mom and Dads taught us that we don't judge people here. Let them dress, walk, live, love, whatever…anyway they want. They are welcome here." Shane turned to him. "Has it changed, Jason?"

Though Jason knew Shane was right, he wasn't about to give him an inch. "McCrae and the others are on my list, Blue. It may be any of them."

"And it might be Kip Lunceford's doing," Shane said flatly.

How the hell does he know that? "What do you mean?"

"Just idle gossip," he said, looking like a kid caught with his hand in the cookie jar. "I heard the guy has really shaken up our town."

"That's putting it mildly," Corey said. "I just got a text from my boss. The fucker has escaped. I've been reassigned to track and apprehend him. They are aware of his interest in Destiny."

"As are we." Joanne Brown, his CIA superior, entered the room, followed by Dylan.

Corey turned to her. "May I ask who you are?"

She held out her hand. "I'm Agent Brown, Marshal. CIA."

He took her hand and shook it. "Since I'm not in uniform, I guess you already have a dossier on me."

"I do. I'm the reason you have been brought in on the Lunceford issue."

"Shane, I need you to leave now." Jason was uncomfortable with all the information flying around the room. "I swear I'll do my best to get whoever is your sister's stalker."

Brown turned to Shane. There was something in her gaze that seemed odd to Jason. Had Brown—with all her fact-finding on everyone else in town—discovered Blue's prison history? Or had these two met before? Maybe at the O'Learys' party before she'd come over to talk to him and Dylan. "Mr. Blue, if you don't mind. I would like to speak with these gentlemen alone."

Shane shrugged and turned to Jason. "Suit yourself. You're my parole officer. As you've been telling me since I came home, I'm supposed to do as you say."

Jason suppressed a smile. "That about covers it."

"Fine." Shane left without another word, closing the door behind him. Odd. Shane wasn't one to give in so easily.

"Blue, you're on my team now."

"I'm no CIA spook, Brown."

"You are now, just like the sheriff." The woman took a seat.

"Don't try to argue with her, Corey. She had the governor call me."

"I'm not tied to the state, so a call from him wouldn't impact me in any way."

"How about a call from the vice president? Would that change your mind, Marshal?" She didn't wait for him to answer, but continued. "Gentlemen, since Black's death, the highest levels of the government have been engaged. Lunceford is considered by everyone to be our greatest domestic threat."

"So what do you have for us?" Dylan asked.

Jason liked his get-to-the-point attitude, always cutting through the crap.

She reached in her briefcase and pulled out several devices. "These are for you. They're highly classified and the latest and greatest to come out of Langley." She handed each of them one.

"What are they?" Jason asked.

"Their technical name is Reconnaissance Oscillating Communication Seven Series, but we call them ROCs."

"Looks more like a cell phone to me," he said.

"That's intentional, but ROCs are much more than that. These are for the others on the team." She placed four more on his desk, keeping one for herself.

"Others?" Corey asked.

"MacCabe, Dixon, Taylor, and the sheriff's deputy, Coleman." Brown looked down at the screen of her tablet. "When you log on, your initial password is your birth year followed by the name of our team, Shannon's Eight."

"Why that name?" Jason asked, knowing Brown had never met her.

"Ms. Day died the same time as Black in the line of duty. Destiny's loss is the Agency's loss, too."

"That's fitting." Corey nodded.

Jason punched in the temporary password and was sent to a prompt to set a new one. "This seems pretty basic, Brown."

"Keep going, Sheriff," she instructed.

Five minutes and several high-tech levels later, including Jason having to place his thumb on the screen for a fingerprint verification, the ROC's contents were finally on its screen.

Brown continued, "As you can see by file zero-one-six-zebra, Mitrofanov has moved the five million into diamonds. His second cousin is a top-tier fence, so it wasn't difficult for him to do."

"Makes sense." Dylan's eyes remained on his own ROC. "Transporting gems is much easier than currency."

She nodded. "The Agency had blocked all the avenues to move the monies electronically."

Jason wanted to catch Mitrofanov and put an end to all the crap that had rained down in Destiny. *My town to protect.* "Where are the diamonds now?"

"Somewhere in the Midwest," she answered. "Word on the street is Mitrofanov owes the Chicago mafia a bundle."

"The Outfit doesn't take kindly to debtors." Corey looked up from his device that Brown had given him. "Niklaus better pay up or they will put the fat fuck in the grave."

"Glad to have you on the team, Marshal," Brown said, vocalizing Jason's sentiments exactly. "I've got eyes and ears on all of Mitrofanov's old gang. No sign of him yet, but once Niklaus pops his head out anywhere, I'll know it."

Jason looked up from his ROC. "Can Lunceford and Mitrofanov's connection to the laptop Black retrieved from Russia help us find both fuckers?"

"My guys back at Langley found more on the device. There was an e-mail exchange we recovered buried deep in the cookies. Took some of our best to put it back together into something we could use."

"And?" Dylan asked.

"Mitrofanov stiffed Lunceford," she answered. "Niklaus was supposed to turn over half the money to Kip, but he never did. The last message from Lunceford to Mitrofanov was he was coming to collect what he was due."

Jason smiled, impressed by Brown's skills. "So, if we find Mitrofanov or the money—we find Kip Lunceford, our primary target."

"You got it, Sheriff."

Moments later, the rest of Shannon's Eight arrived.

After Nicole, Matt, Sean, and Jena were brought up to speed, Brown finished the briefing. "Once we get a lock on anything, I will send Dylan, Matt, and Sean to extract our targets."

Mitrofanov had made Jason's life hell the past several months. He wasn't about to miss seeing the motherfucker's arrest. "I want to be part of that mission, Brown."

"I was hoping you would." After she advised them what the next steps would be in the mission, now dubbed Diamond Sweep, the meeting ended.

They all shook each other's hands. They were a team now with a common enemy. It felt good to be part of such a capable group.

Jason turned to their new boss. "Brown, could I speak with you for a moment?"

"What's up, Sheriff?"

"Dylan has been helping me with a stalker situation, but I think you have more resources than he does."

"Not sure I can help you with local issues, Jason."

"It might not be local. In fact, it might actually help with this mission."

She raised her eyebrows. "How?"

"I have reason to believe the stalker might be Kip Lunceford."

Chapter Eight

Phoebe held Lucas's hand as they stood outside the chapel. He'd just returned from his overnight stay at the Boys Ranch. She'd enjoyed her time with Mitchell, but she'd missed Lucas. "I'm so glad Jena wanted to be married here." They'd arrived early with Mitchell, since his band was providing the music. Wolfe Mayhem was inside setting up.

Gazing at the view from this elevation, she could see Destiny down below. "It's absolutely breathtaking. I love your chapel."

He looked stunning in his suit and cowboy boots. "Thank you, baby. I love it, too."

"I remember you showing me drawings of it on a napkin at my parents' diner when we were still in high school."

"I still have them."

She squeezed his hand. "This is your dream come true."

"Yes, it is, but the real dream for me is you, Phoebe. Being with you forever."

She kissed him on the steps of the little brick chapel he'd designed. "Let's go inside."

"After you, honey." He opened the door for her.

"Lucas, it's even more beautiful inside," she said, gazing at the all-white interior, coupled with warm neutrals and cool grays. The place looked heavenly. "I love your chapel."

He smiled broadly. "It's not mine, baby. It's Destiny's, hence the name."

"Destiny's Little Mountain Chapel. Nice name."

"Ethel's choice. She's funding all my buildings, except for the

Boys Ranch and the Clinic. She gets to pick the names."

"The town has never looked better." Her pride for Lucas was enormous. "Your fingerprints are everywhere. The renovations and the new buildings are going to make Destiny the jewel of Colorado."

Mitchell stood next to Big Jim by the mixer.

Godric and Hank were strapping on their instruments.

Kaylyn stood by a microphone. "Test. Test. Test."

Phoebe couldn't wait to hear the band play Mitchell's sound. She was so proud of him.

Being an hour before the ceremony and seeing no ushers around, Lucas led her up the aisle. They took their seats.

"Hey, sweetheart," Mitchell said after spotting her. "That's my girl," he told the band.

"Phoebe, you look so happy," Kaylyn said with a grin. "I love that you're wearing your hair down."

"Where's your mom?" She knew that Betty had to be close, being the town's most sought after stylist, especially when it came to weddings.

"With Jena in the bridal room, doing touch ups. Mom is going to be thrilled when she sees you."

"She's been begging me to style it down all the time, but for the courtroom, I prefer wearing it up."

"I wouldn't fight with Betty, if I were you," Mitchell said. "Besides, you look amazing letting it fall to your shoulders."

"I have to agree," Lucas said. He turned his attention to Mitchell. "By the way, didn't you mean *our* girl, bro?" He smiled and put his arm around her.

Mitchell nodded. "I stand corrected. Our girl."

"Better, Mitch. Much better."

If only Jason was here, too—on the same page.

Doubts swarmed in her head. Mitchell and Lucas had come around quickly enough, letting go of the past and grabbing onto the possibility of a future. Making love to each of them had been so freeing, so right. But Jason was all about the rules. He'd proven that again and again. Would he be able to move on from the hurt she'd inflicted on all of them?

"For our warm-up, let's play number five from the set list for the reception. I want Phoebe to hear it."

Though she didn't know what song he'd chosen, it was clearly the one that would showcase the sound he'd finally found. *Our sound.*

When the band started, she immediately heard the difference. Kaylyn's voice blended to perfection with the rest of the band. Not to even mention the beautiful words Mitchell had written. Her heart soared with every beat, every syllable, every note.

"…you belong with me, my love, in my arms under the stars of Destiny," Kaylyn's final note reverberated through the chapel.

The hairs of her arms stood up from the sound she'd just enjoyed. She ran up to Mitchell, unable to contain herself.

"I love our sound." She grabbed him and kissed him.

The band applauded their approval.

She gazed into Mitchell's eyes. He bent down and kissed her again.

"Whose wedding is this anyway?" Hank's teasing tone brought her back to her senses.

She broke free of the kiss. As she turned to go to her seat, she saw Jason standing in the back in his sheriff's uniform, looking confused and angry.

He saw the whole thing. Before she had a chance to go to him and explain, Jason turned and walked out. *What am I to do?*

* * * *

Exiting the chapel, Jason's heart shattered. *Phoebe wants my brothers but not me. Why am I being left out?*

Several cars pulled into the tiny parking lot, so he walked to the side of the building. He needed time to think, to be alone.

He hadn't been sure he would make the wedding at all since he'd been swamped with his regular duties and Brown's mission to find Lunceford.

Kaylyn had called him, making him promise to show up no matter what. She wanted him to hear her sing with Mitchell's band. Here he was in his uniform, but now he wished he hadn't come at all.

When he'd seen Lucas sitting in the pew next to her, his gut clenched. When she'd walked up to Mitchell and kissed him, he felt like his whole world was being ripped apart.

Doesn't she know I love her?

How could she know? He'd been so cold to her ever since the breakup.

It's all my fault.

She would never be able to forgive him. It would be best for him to just fade into the background and let her have a future with his brothers. He could picture them having a happy life together—Phoebe in between Lucas and Mitchell, walking around town, smiling and holding their children's hands.

I could never face that. The last three years without her had been horrible, but seeing her in the arms of his brothers without him—that would be tragedy.

I won't be able to stay here. I will have to leave Destiny and my brothers. I will have to leave Phoebe.

He curled his hands into fists and closed his eyes. How long he stayed that way, he wasn't sure. Seconds? Minutes? Who knew? Every moment without her was like an eternity of emptiness.

The sound of the wedding march started up.

Not wanting to think anymore about the hell he was facing, Jason walked back into the chapel. The place was packed to standing room only. He moved to one of the columns in the back, his eyes zeroing in on Phoebe, still sitting by Lucas.

Mitchell and his band played *When I Fall In Love*, one of the standards they always performed at weddings. But Jason had never heard it sung by Wolfe Mayhem's new lead singer, Kaylyn. Her voice was like an angel and reached deep into him, transporting him back to a time when he'd dreamed of being with Phoebe forever, of sharing the love of his life with his brothers.

His gaze never left Phoebe, even when Jena shared her personal wedding vows to Matt and Sean, her two grooms. The trio were outsiders, new to Destiny, but had found love. *Why can't I have my dream?* Growing up here, he'd fallen for Phoebe so long ago that he couldn't remember a time not loving her.

As Matt began his vows, Jason's mind drifted to the wedding talk with Phoebe and his brothers. He could picture the whole thing in his mind. He would stand in between his brothers facing their bride, the most beautiful woman in the world.

Suddenly, the band fired up the wedding recessional tune, snapping him out of his thoughts.

The service was over.

He wasn't the groom.

This wasn't his wedding.

Phoebe wasn't his wife.

As the attendees turned to watch the new family head down the aisle, his eyes locked with the woman of his dreams for a moment.

She wasn't his. Not anymore. Not for a long time.

He broke free of her stare.

Phoebe deserved a chance at happiness.

Lucas and Mitchell will give her a good life.

He slipped out the back, once again, needing time alone—time to think.

* * * *

Phoebe couldn't hold back her trembles. Seeing Jason walk out the back door of the chapel crushed her heart.

"What's wrong?" Lucas whispered, pulling her in close.

"Jason saw me kissing Mitchell. I didn't know what to do."

"I'm sure he's confused and upset."

"But he left. Lucas, we've got to go talk to him."

"*We* don't. *You* do," he said. "You need your time with him alone. I will take you, but I will stay in the background. Let's tell Mitchell what we're doing and then I'll take you to Jason's office."

"That's not where he's going."

"No?"

She shook her head, knowing exactly where he'd gone. The first time Jason had taken her to his secret place, they'd just been teenagers. The last time she'd gone there to find him was to break up with him. Would he be able to forgive her? With all her heart, she hoped he would. She loved him.

Without Jason she wasn't sure how she would survive.

* * * *

As they arrived at the lake, Phoebe was so anxious, she jumped out of the car. "Lucas, I'll be back. Just wait here."

She walked down the path of the familiar place, her mind racing for some way to make Jason understand how sorry she was for everything. Would he forgive her? Would he believe her when she told him she loved him—had always loved him?

Rounding the corner, she saw Jason by his favorite tree, head down, bent over.

Her heart racing and overcome with emotion, she ran to him.

He looked up, his eyes full of concern. "Phoebe?"

She kissed him deeply, all the words she planned vanishing into thin air. "Oh, Jason. I'm so sorry. I was such a fool. I've never stopped loving you. Please forgive me."

Jason placed his fingers on her lips. "Shh, baby. I was the fool, not you. I have treated you so badly the past three years. My foolish pride got in the way of our happiness together."

"No," she said, shaking her head. "It was me. I was the stubborn one. When I saw you in the chapel after I kissed Mitchell, my heart broke because we were not all together the way we always planned."

"No, I was the stubborn one."

"No, I was."

"Was not," he said with a grin. "I was."

"Can we both agree that we each had a hand in it, Sheriff?"

He pulled her in close. "As long as I get to have you in my arms, I'll agree to anything, honey."

Chapter Nine

Jason walked back to his patrol car, holding onto Phoebe. He was happy. Really happy. They headed over to Lucas. It was the first time since the breakup that he'd seen his middle brother smiling.

"It's obvious you two worked things out quite nicely," Lucas said.

Though Jason and his brothers had been with her many times in the past, they'd never shared her in the bedroom. It wasn't that they weren't open to the idea. They'd grown up in Destiny. They were open to a lot of ideas, especially sexual exploration. An opportunity to make love to her together had just never presented itself, especially with each of them having different tours of duty in different branches of the military. Later, Phoebe had been starting her practice. Mitchell had been traveling with his band. Lucas's job had been demanding due to the many projects he led around the state. And Jason had been in the thick of Destiny politics with plans on running for Sheriff Grayson's position once the man retired. So, their lovemaking with her had been one-on-one.

"There's more to talk through, but yes, we did." Phoebe leaned her head into his chest.

"I'm taking her home." Though he was glad that he was going to get to share this amazing woman with his two brothers, he was still pissed that they'd left him out of the loop about the recent stalker events.

Lucas nodded. "Sounds good to me."

At long last, they were all finally getting past what had happened three years ago, but he knew there was a lot of air that still needed to be cleared. That would have to wait for another time. "Lucas, we'll talk later." Right, now, he only wanted to get Phoebe home and make love to her until the sun came up.

"Absolutely. Now that we have her back, we have a lot to discuss, I'm sure."

More than you know, bro. More than you know.

Phoebe moved forward and wrapped her arms around Lucas. She kissed him. "Thank you for helping me. I love you."

"I love you, too." Lucas got in his car and drove away.

With rosy pink cheeks, Phoebe stepped up to him. "I missed you, Jason. I missed you so very much."

He inhaled her scent of jasmine. "My life has never been the same since the breakup, sweetheart."

"Really, this is all my fault. I've talked to Lucas and Mitchell already. I understand why you three did what you did with Shane."

"Do you?" he asked, knowing she had no clue what had gone down between him and Shane at the diner that day. No one did.

"I'm his sister. Can you understand why I acted the way I did?"

"I understand much more than you can imagine, baby."

She blinked, reminding him of her submissive side he'd enjoyed time and again before the breakup. "Can you ever forgive me, Jason?"

He stroked her hair away from her eyes. "That's about enough of that."

Her lips began to tremble. "We lost three years because of me. Me. I–I…can't forgive myself. Please say something."

He stepped back an arm's length from her. "Sub, are you listening to me?"

Her eyes widened, but she responded beautifully. "Yes, Sir."

"You've been away from me too long. I told you to let it go but you kept going."

"B–But—"

"Stop. Listen." He paused, taking a hard look at the most incredible woman he'd ever known. Independent. Capable. Honest. Loyal. And a whole slew of other characteristics that just made him love her all the more. "Better. You've been without a Dom's firm hand for a very long time. I was going to wait until we got back to your place, but I see you need a refresher right away."

"A refresher?"

"Excuse me," he said in his most commanding tone.

She looked puzzled for a split second and then she smiled, realizing what he had in store for her. "Sir, what kind of refresher?"

She was getting into it quite nicely, and that was making his cock stir.

He reached out and touched her cheek, gazing into her eyes. "You already know.

She nodded. "Yes, Sir. I do."

"Stretch out on the hood of my car. Face down."

"Sir, I'm in the dress I wore to the wedding. It's expensive."

He growled his discontent. "Now."

She sent him a devilish grin and then obeyed him.

He would have her dress cleaned and would even buy her several new ones. His three years of suffering and loneliness were over. His longing for her had never ceased, held back by his vow to do whatever made her find happiness. He'd thought that meant staying out of her life. Now, he knew that she needed him as much as he needed her, and that awakened every part of his being. He felt more alive than he had in years. His desire for her flooded his body.

"Lift your dress," he commanded.

Again, she didn't hesitate one second, pulling it up so it would expose her thong.

He ripped it off of her, enjoying her gasp followed by tiny moans. She was getting turned on.

He placed his hand on her round ass. "Your hard edge safe word is *freeze*, right?"

"Yes, Sir. You remember. I'm so glad."

He bent down and kissed both her cheeks, enjoying the softness of her ass's skin. "I remember everything, sub. I remember you trembling at my feet after I'd spanked this sweet ass of mine. It's still mine, pet. You understand that, don't you?"

"Yes, Sir."

He reached under her until his fingers were on her sweet pussy, which was already wet, making his cock stand up and salute. "This is mine, too."

"Your pussy, Sir. Yes. I understand."

He skimmed his fingers down her legs, loving the heat he felt from her skin. "Baby, you need a spanking in the worst way. I wish I had a paddle with me, but I don't. You're going to have to settle for my open hand. You think that will be enough to get your attention, sub?"

"Yes, Sir," she whispered, turning her head just enough so he could get a look at her beautiful wide blue eyes.

He remembered the first time he'd used a crop on her and how her cream had run down her legs. The memories of her surrendering all of herself to him, again and again, burned fresh in his mind. His balls ached and his cock throbbed.

He shook his head, trying to keep a rein on his three-year frustration of being without her, without the love of his life. She was his world. He'd let her walk away without a fight. There would be no way in heaven on earth or in hell he would ever let that happen again.

She needed him to take things slow and easy. She'd been to Phase Four a few times after the breakup, but she'd not been with any other Doms there. That pleased him very much. Now that he had her under his power, he couldn't let his desires override what he knew she needed from him.

"You've been blaming yourself for far too long about what happened. That's why I have you up on my car. That's why I'm going to spank you. I tried to get you to let it go, but you wouldn't. Now, I'm going to help you let it go. Understand?"

"Yes, Sir."

"Time to get this ass of mine nice and warm."

"Shall I count, Sir?"

Same wonderful, saucy Phoebe. I'm the one who is going to be her slave, not the other way around. "Yes, sub. Count for me."

"I would love to," she said, her voice full of seductive excitement and playful sassiness.

For so many years, her words had been clipped and harsh. Now, hearing her talk to him the way she used to, open and soft, his need to possess and claim her again as his own overtook him. Only one woman had ever satisfied him and made him feel whole—Phoebe Blue, the woman with the heart of a lion and the body of a goddess.

He'd found her long ago, but had let her slip through his fingers. He'd confessed his undying love to her by *his* tree, not thirty feet from here. They'd grown up together. He'd been only a boy and she'd been only an innocent girl.

Now, they were man and woman. Flesh and blood. They belonged together. Life had taken an unwanted detour, but now they were on the road again, headed to a forever he knew would be filled with more joy than he could ever imagine.

The image of her standing in front of him and his brothers at the chapel returned. They would be married. They would have a family, children. They would walk the streets of Destiny, arm in arm, for the rest of their lives.

She looked up at him. "Sir?"

"Yes, sub?"

"How many?"

"God, I love you," he confessed. "I remember how impatient you can be, sub."

"I apologize, Sir." She smiled but he knew she wasn't sorry even a little. She always did love to push him in play. That was just one of the things he adored about her. "I love you, too."

"I love everything about you, baby. I still have to spank you, understand?"

"Yes, Sir. I should be spanked." She gave him a sexy look that ramped up his hunger for her even more. "I've been so very bad."

She needed to be reminded that he was in charge.

"No you don't," he scolded, unable to hold back his smile. "No topping me from the bottom, baby."

* * * *

In the unseasonably warm air, Phoebe squirmed on Jason's patrol car, the pressure mounting with every syllable that came out of his mouth.

Jason's hot gaze got her wetter. "I'm the one who decides when and how many whacks to this perfect ass need to be rained down, not you."

"Please," she begged him, remembering how much he'd liked it when she did. "I'm sorry, Sir, but I'm burning inside for you."

"You'll be burning on the outside pretty soon, too." He trailed his hands up and down her body, starting at her neck, down her back, to her bottom, down her legs, and ending at her feet. "You're extremely sensitive here. I remember." He traced his fingers over her toes, causing her to jump.

She giggled uncontrollably at his tickle torture. Goose bumps popped up on her skin. Now that he'd opened the gate to laughter, there was no going back. Every inch of her became hypersensitive to his touch.

His deep, gleeful laugh mixed with hers as he ran his fingers up her sides, sending her into a state of hysterics. Could anyone hear her? Since they were so far away from town, she didn't think so. But as loud as she and Jason were laughing, she bet any wildlife around would be scared away. Imagining bears, bunnies, and deer scurrying down the mountain to escape her sent her into another bout of roaring laughter.

"Now, you're ready for your spanking, sweetheart." Jason landed his hand on the center of her ass, capturing all her attention and turning her giggles into dreamy moans.

She felt the burn he'd delivered to her bottom start to spread through the rest of her body. She remembered he'd told her to count aloud. "One, Sir."

"Very good, my little sub." Jason's praise filled her with pride. "Four more to go."

Four? Nervous and excited, she curled her hands into fists.

The slap of his hand sizzled on her left cheek.

"Two, Sir." She was on fire and loving it, loving him, loving being with him again. This was where she belonged. Jason, though flesh and blood, was more home to her than her house. With him, she felt loved and protected.

The next whack hit her right cheek, making her wonderfully dizzy.

"Three, Sir." She was once again gliding into a state of bliss that he'd taken her to long ago.

The next two whacks landed back to back in the center of her ass, and then she felt the soft edges of the trance she'd missed for far too long. "Four. Five."

He lifted her off the hood of his car. When he lowered her to her feet, she leaned up and wrapped her arms around his neck. "Thank you." Tears welled in her eyes. This was where she belonged. *With Jason.*

"You're mine, Phoebe Blue. You will always be mine."

"Yes, Sir." With her mind relaxed and dreamy, she could just be. There were no tasks to concern herself with, no worries to trouble her. In this state, all that mattered was being with him. With Jason. With Sir.

She felt him reach behind her, pulling her strapless dress's zipper down slow, tortuously slow. Unable to contain herself, she began unbuttoning his shirt.

Smiling, he caught her wrists in his hands. "There you go again, sub. Trying to take charge."

She could see in his dark eyes wicked hunger, and that made her tremble. That he was able to keep his passion contained stunned her. His willpower amazed her. She was ready to rip his clothes off.

She needed him inside her, needed to be filled by him, needed to give herself to him. "Please, Sir. I want you. The pressure is too much. I can't take more. It's been so long."

He narrowed his eyes, keeping hold of her wrists with one hand. "Oh but you will take more, baby. Much more. You will take all I want to give you. When I'm sure you've had enough and I believe you've earned your reward, then I'll end your suffering, pet." He placed his handcuffs on her, a clear act of his dominance over her. "You will stand there and watch me take my clothes off."

"Yes, Sir." *God, yes. I want to see your body again, Jason.*

He took his time undressing. He emptied his pockets of his keys and wallet, placing them on the front seat of his car, along with his gun and belt. A cool breeze rolled over her skin, reminding her they were exposed and in the open. Her shivers were not from being outside but from the internal fire building inside her.

When he finally removed his shirt, she saw the white T-shirt that covered his perfectly muscled frame.

How long is he going to take? As if they had minds of their own, her cuffed hands stretched out to assist him.

Jason stepped back, just out of fingertip range. "No you don't, sub." He brought his hands to her breasts, pinching both nipples. "You will wait. Do you understand me?"

"Yes, Sir," she answered, lowering her gaze from the big bad Dom in front of her. *My big bad Dom.* Her nipples throbbed, creating a warm sphere of sensations in her chest that spread down her abdomen, landing between her legs. Her clit began to tingle. *How much longer?* She couldn't take much more. *I need him.*

After several long, agonizing seconds, he removed the last of his clothing—his pants—stepping back just far enough to prevent her from reaching him. He fisted his monstrous cock.

This is torture. She so desperately needed him inside her pussy.

"Look at me," he commanded.

She moved her gaze from his dick up to his dark Dom eyes.

He cupped her chin. "You're trouble, Phoebe Blue. A whole ton of trouble, but that's exactly how I want you to be." He pulled her dress down her body. She stepped free of the outfit and he placed it next to his uniform. She felt another round of wonderful trembles roll through her.

He pinched her nipple lightly, causing her to gasp and arch her back. Her pussy clenched, reminding her how much she wanted him inside her.

He lifted her back onto the car into a sitting position, facing him. He bent down between her legs.

She could feel the heat of his breath on her pussy and that multiplied the pressure inside her.

"I want to taste you, baby." He sent his fingers over her slit, sending a sea of sizzles along her veins. "God, you're soaking wet. I want my mouth on this soft pussy."

Without warning, he kissed her throbbing clit, and she could not contain herself any longer. She shifted her hips forward into his greedy mouth. This time, he didn't make her suffer, but instead bathed her pussy with his tongue. His hands cupped her ass, which was still warm from the spanking he'd given her. She was reaching her limit. She put her hands, still in the cuffs, over his head and felt the spasms coming.

"Give me your cream, baby," his deep voice rumbled, making her shiver even more. "Every single drop." He sucked on her clit as her orgasm swamped every cell in her body.

"Yes. Yes. Yes." Liquid poured out of her pussy as the climax rose higher and higher, stronger and stronger. "Oh God."

Jason's wicked mouth continued working her into a frenzied state. She shook violently as the incredible relief he'd given her burned through her. Every part of her had been taken over completely by one orgasm on top of another.

She closed her eyes, lingering on the surface of the final trembles of her climax. She could feel Jason, removing the handcuffs and then rubbing her wrists.

His deep voice boomed. "Open your eyes, sub."

Instantly, she obeyed. "Yes, Sir." She'd suffered for three years for no reason. This was where she belonged, with Jason.

He pulled her off the car and in so very close, until she could feel his thick, hard cock pressing against her body. His lips ravaged her mouth until her toes curled and the pressure began to build again. Jason's intensity consumed everything in its path. There was no way to avoid his delicious onslaught, not that she would ever want to.

"On your knees," he commanded.

She instantly obeyed him. Pleasing him now was all that mattered.

"I want to feel that pretty mouth of yours around my dick." He stroked her hair. "Lick your lips. Get them nice and wet for me, sub."

"Yes, Sir."

"You want to suck my cock, don't you?"

She moaned. "More than anything, Sir. Please. I want to so badly."

His eyes burned brightly. "God, I'm going to spoil you rotten. So are my brothers. You're going to have us wrapped around your finger if we're not careful." Jason shook his head. "But don't you worry that pretty head of yours, sub. I'm very careful. I'm your Dom. And what are you?"

"I'm your sub, Sir," she confessed. "I'm yours."

"Fuck, yes, you're mine."

"Please let me suck on your cock, Sir. If I do a good job, won't you send it into my pussy?"

His quick grin caused her heart to skip a beat. "We'll see, baby. Make me feel your want in your hot little lips. If you do, I will reward you and fill you with my dick."

Thirsty for him, she parted her lips and brought out her tongue to the head of his cock. She tasted the pearly drop that rested on his slit.

She drank it down, knowing there was more to come. Opening her mouth as wide as she could, she swallowed his dick until it hit the back of her throat. Bringing up her hands to his balls and shaft, she bobbed up and down his cock.

He moaned as she continued sucking on him. When he brought his hands to the back of her head, her pussy began to burn and her clit began to throb once again. She'd never felt such need in all her life. Was it the three years without him that drove her mad with desire?

Yes. God yes.

Tightening her lips until they created a seal between him and her, she sucked hard, hollowing out her cheeks.

"Slow down, baby. I want to get inside you, but I need to get a condom out of my pocket."

No.

She released him. "No condom, Sir."

The puzzled look of frustration on his face troubled her.

She needed him to understand. She needed him inside her. Needed his seed. If this was the night before her forever with the Wolfes began, that's what had to happen. Lucas and Mitchell had made love to her without protection. *He must, too.* "Please. I beg you, Sir."

"I get it, baby." Jason clearly was able to read her mind.

He helped her up off the ground and leaned her on the car. Without another word, his big hands moved down her sides and to her hips. She could feel him shift until the head of his cock was in position to claim her pussy. The first thrust into her body drowned her with utter passion. He shoved his dick into her, lengthening his thrusts with each pass, bit by bit. She tried to shift her hips to take even more of his dick, but Jason, in full-on Dom mode, held her firmly.

"Please. I need you. Don't make me wait. Fill me." Her steamy words would not be contained. They came one after another, her need setting them free.

"I will, baby. I will." He continued thrusting into her, claiming more of her with every stroke. Her entire body was full of him and still the pressure grew and grew.

"Oh God," she said on the brink of release.

"Your pussy is so tight, you're killing me," he told her. "God, you feel so fucking good."

She felt her insides tighten around his thick shaft. Ripples, one after the other, from deep within exploded out of her.

"Come for me, sub. That's it. You're close, aren't you? God, knows I'm about to come inside this gorgeous body, baby."

She squeezed her thighs as tight as she could as his thrusts hit that sensitive spot in her channel. She couldn't stay still. Everything inside her was burning and shaking. She arched her body into his, accepting more of his thickness.

"Fuck, yeah." His hot stare never left her, but she could see his face tighten for a bit. "Yes."

He was impossibly deep inside her, and yet he plunged even deeper still in one final, overwhelming thrust.

Feeling him shoot his seed into her body, she screamed and he groaned. The trembles went on and on and she hoped they would never end.

With his cock still inside her, he pulled her in tight into his muscled frame. "God, that was one for the record books, baby."

She giggled. "Shall I call Guinness, Sir?"

He laughed and picked her up. "You will never learn, will you?"

"What do you mean?"

"You're about to find out." He carried her to the lake and threw her in, jumping in after her. The temperature was warmer than normal for this time of year. The cool water felt good on her skin. She broke the surface, laughing.

"No one jumps in the water in November." She splashed water right into his face. "That's for throwing me in."

"It's on, girl." He splashed her back, beginning their latest water fight.

She ran out of the water and grabbed his uniform. "Jason Wolfe, you're about to find out what I'm capable of, too."

His grinned. "You wouldn't dare."

"Oh no." She chunked them into the lake, dying of laughter before jumping back in.

"Fair is fair, baby." He ran out of the water and grabbed her clothes.

"Jason, I'm sorry," she said as sweetly as she could. "Please. That really is an expensive outfit."

"Is it?" He winked and got his keys from the seat of the car. He opened the trunk and put the dress inside.

"Jason, I can't go back to town without my clothes."

"Really? But you expect me to?" He laughed and slammed the lid down, locking her dress away.

"Now you're going to pay for that, mister." She swam back a bit from the shore. "Just try to get me and see what happens."

"I forgot how much I loved your sass, baby." He dove in and the war continued.

Exhausted after several battles, he carried her back to the car. "I love you, Phoebe."

She placed a hand on his cheek, enjoying the feel of his stubble on her fingertips. "I love you, Jason, but you better not have caused me to catch a cold."

"There's that sass I so love." He kissed her, helping her to remember how wonderful a man he was.

Chapter Ten

As they crossed over Silver Spoon Bridge, Phoebe leaned down low into Jason's naked body. "Can you imagine what your chances of being reelected are if anyone sees us?"

He laughed. "Not good. I can see the headlines of the *Destiny Daily* tomorrow. 'In the buff, sheriff and attorney are caught joyriding around town.'"

"I hope you don't have to pull anyone over for speeding. That'll ruin everything."

He died laughing and she joined in. "I think I'll turn on my lights and siren on the way to your house, baby."

"Don't you dare, Jason."

He kissed her wet hair. "I have such fun with you."

"Me, too. No one can make me laugh like you."

He pulled up into her driveway. The streetlight illuminated her porch, so tiptoeing was out. They would have to make a dash to her front door or else her neighbors would get an eyeful.

"Ready, baby?"

"I can't find my keys," she said, rifling through her purse.

"I can break down the door if necessary," he said, grabbing his cell and gun and some other device.

"Are you so bent on making sure someone sees us? No commotion. Please. I have to live on this street. Found them. Let me get your clothes. I'll throw them in the dryer." With his uniform in one hand and her keys in the other, she opened her car door. "Last one inside has to make the drinks while the other one cleans up."

Not waiting for an answer, she sprinted to her door.

Jason passed her, blocking her way. "You don't play fair, Phoebe Blue."

"Look who's talking?" She saw one of her neighbor's porch lights come on and she froze. "Jason, please."

He laughed. "I do like being sheriff. Maybe I should go see if there's something your neighbors need."

"I beg you, don't."

"Give me the keys."

"Do you always have to win?"

"You know me quite well. You tell me."

"Fine." She handed him her keys, and he put his arm around her. "You win."

When they headed up her sidewalk, she heard the lady next door say, "Is everything all right, Phoebe?"

"Yes, Mrs. Handley. Everything is fine." She giggled. *Everything is perfect.* "Goodnight."

"She voted for my opponent, Phoebe. We need to get inside."

"What? Are you worried she'll ruin your next election, Sheriff?" He grinned. "You know how the politics can get crazy here. Yes, she can. Let's go."

They came up the steps of her front porch. A vase of red roses was at the foot of her door. "These must be from one of your brothers."

"My money is on Mitchell. He's the most sensitive of the three of us."

"Musicians always are." She bent down to retrieve the vase as Jason put the key in the door. "It might be from Lucas or both of them. You never sent me flowers, Jason. A girl likes getting flowers you know."

He cupped her ass and led her inside. "I know exactly what this girl likes and you know it."

"Devil."

"Vixen," he said with a laugh. "Well? Which brother are these from?"

She opened the tiny envelope and felt her heart seize. "It's from *him*. From the stalker."

* * * *

Jason's body tensed. He took the card from Phoebe's trembling fingers. Reading the message filled him with protective rage.

You looked beautiful at the wedding today, Phoebe. You have no idea how much you mean to me. Please stay away from the Wolfe brothers. I wouldn't want anything bad to happen to them.
Love,
Your Secret Admirer.

He held her close. "It's going to be okay, baby. Trust me."

"I do, but this is so crazy."

"You let me handle crazy. You stay put while I check out the house."

She nodded.

With his gun out, he checked every nook and cranny of her place. The fucker wasn't here and there was no sign that he'd ever been.

"We're alone, honey." He put his arm around her. "Let's get you in a warm bath. I will take care of everything."

"Thank you. I don't know what I would do without you."

He filled the tub. "I'll bring you a glass of wine and something to nibble on after I make a few calls."

She slipped into the water. "Who do you think this guy is, Jason?"

"Honey, it's too early to say."

"Please. I know you have some ideas."

"It might be Andy McCrae," he admitted.

"If it is, then my worries are over. He's harmless."

He wasn't about to remind her that the stalker had hacked into both his brothers' phones. *Definitely not harmless.* "When was the last time you saw him?"

"A year ago, at least. But who else could it be? You have other suspects, don't you?"

"Yes. I'm worried that Mitrofanov or Lunceford or both might be pulling the strings on this, baby. Until I know for certain, you will not be left alone."

She smiled. "You three are more alike than you think."

He kissed her. "When it comes to your safety, we are in total agreement. Relax. I'll be back in a few minutes to check on you." He exited, leaving the door to the bathroom open.

He walked into the living room with his cell and ROC in one hand and his gun in the other. He brought the phone up to his ear. Looking around her place, he spotted so many items and photos that reminded him of how their life had once been. *It's going to be again.*

Two rings later, Lucas answered. "Hey, Jason. How's our girl?"

"She just got flowers delivered from the stalker."

"I'll be there in five minutes. I'll call Mitchell on the way. The wedding reception just ended. He's packing up the equipment."

Jason hung up the phone.

After putting his wet clothes in her dryer, he walked into Phoebe's kitchen. Next to a couple of bottles of merlot, which he knew to be her preference, he found an unopened bottle of Jack Daniels, his favorite drink. Phoebe didn't drink hard liquor. Ever. Beer or wine were as strong as she drank. Why did she keep a bottle of Jack on hand? In his heart, he knew why. *For me. She keeps it for me.*

He got out a couple of glasses and poured each of them a drink. He'd finally seen the old smile on her face tonight, and that had sent his heart soaring. No fucking psycho was going to harm a single hair on her head. He'd give his life, if necessary, to make sure she remained safe.

What if the stalker turns out to be Kip Lunceford? He drank the entire contents in his glass, sending the biting whiskey down his throat.

He fired up his ROC that Brown had given him and the rest of her new team.

Lunceford had escaped. Was he Phoebe's stalker? Even if he were, Kip would be a fool to come to Destiny for Phoebe. And a question kept swimming around in his head. *Why her?*

She and Lunceford had little connection. Sure, the maniac loved pulling strings, especially when it came to the Knights. Megan, their wife, was Kip's ex. Lunceford even liked screwing with the whole town. But it just didn't make sense that he would zero in on Phoebe.

Looking at the files Brown had already shown him, he poured another shot. "What am I missing? What don't I know about this?" Rage still simmered close to the surface inside him. He looked at the flowers. They'd come from a florist, so there likely wouldn't be prints of any use on the vase. The florist was located in Clover, about ten miles from Destiny. Perhaps there were prints on the note, though. Also, there might be a possibility the florist saw the son of bitch's face. He'd go with Nicole to Clover to check that out first thing in the morning.

He slammed the roses into the trash. There had been fear in Phoebe's eyes when she'd read the card. He cursed under his breath.

With the glass of merlot and a plate of fruit, cheese, and crackers, he walked back into where he'd left her.

From the tub, she looked up at him. "What can we do about this stalker issue?"

He smiled. "You haven't changed a bit, baby."

"What do you mean?"

"Always straight to the point. This is what you're going to do. You will enjoy your bath." He grabbed a towel and put it around his waist. "And I am going to take care of everything. Understand?"

She nodded. "I'm glad you're here, Jason."

He'd always been awed by her courage, but never more than now. The last three years had been tough on him but even more so on her. She'd seen her brother fall hard and land in prison. She'd walked away from love, and he and his brothers had let her go. No matter what kind of knocks life dished out to her, she kept getting up, kept fighting.

Whoever the creep turned out to be, Jason would make sure the psycho never bothered her again. Breaking any law was something he'd never thought possible for him. But now, he knew whatever it took to make sure Phoebe was safe he would do, including killing the motherfucker, with or without legal cause.

His cell rang and Phoebe's eyes widened. He looked at the screen. "It's not him, baby. Relax." The caller was Agent Brown.

Her shoulders sagged. "I guess I'm just a bit jumpy," she said, taking a sip of wine.

"Understandable." He put the phone to his ear. "Hello."

"We got a hit on your stalker issue, Jason," Brown said. "We know who he is."

Chapter Eleven

Lucas bolted past Jason, who had opened Phoebe's front door for him. "Where is she?"

"Getting dressed in her bedroom." With only a towel around his waist, Jason held a phone to his ear. "She's fine. Go see for yourself."

Lucas found her sitting on her bed in a robe. "Baby, are you all right?"

"I'm okay." Phoebe's trembling hands told him she was nervous.

He put his arms around her and held her tightly. "It's going to be okay, sweetheart. I'm sure Jason has a plan started already. We'll have this guy before you know it. In the meantime, we will be by your side at all times."

"I got here as fast as I could." Mitchell's words came from the other room, as did Jason's.

"She's with Lucas in the bedroom, Mitch."

He and Phoebe met Mitchell in the hallway.

She wrapped her arms around Mitchell. "All three of you are here. For me." Her voice shook.

The three of them returned to the living room where Jason was now dressed and still on the phone.

Lucas wondered who was on the other end of the call.

"I'll let you know what I find out in Clover tomorrow." Jason clicked off his phone. "I've got news. That was Mr. Black's replacement, Agent Brown. I asked her to help me on the stalker issue."

"Bringing in the CIA is a good thing." The serious tone in Mitchell's voice was unusual, but given what was going on was about

Phoebe, it was not unexpected. "What did she say?"

Jason stepped in front of Phoebe. "Turns out that Andy McCrae is your stalker."

"I can't believe it." She shook her head. "He might be strange, but I actually feel better knowing it's him. Andy couldn't harm a fly."

"How does Brown know it's him?" Lucas still thought the SOB needed to have his face pounded into the ground. Any man who harassed women deserved that and much more. McCrae hadn't stalked just any woman. He'd stalked Phoebe.

"You've heard about what the Feds can do with phone records. Dylan had run all of the calls Phoebe had received through his channels. Nothing. Brown stepped it up several notches. She's got quite the pull. We got a hit. One of the calls came from a burner phone that McCrae purchased with his credit card."

Mitchell snorted. "Not too smart."

"Criminals always screw up in the end." Jason touched Phoebe's cheek.

"What an idiot." Lucas remembered how the TBK tech appeared around town. He looked more like a deadbeat loser, with his long stringy hair that always seemed in need of shampoo, than a brilliant engineer.

"I doubt he was expecting the CIA to get involved." Jason patted his gun, which was holstered to his side. He meant business, deadly business. "Besides, all the other cells McCrae bought weren't purchased with credit cards."

Mitchell nodded. "It's good for our team that the bastard finally slipped up then."

Jason continued. "Brown hit all the databases at the Agency. More credit card transactions popped up. McCrae has been in and out of the county for weeks, mainly staying at the motel in Clover."

Phoebe sighed but her trembling had stopped. She was strong and brave. "That's only ten miles from Destiny."

Mitchell turned to Lucas. "No wonder the fucker knew to call you and me when we came to her house."

"He's a tech. Getting our numbers would be simple for him." Lucas held Phoebe's hand and squeezed. "The rat must've been skulking around town and scurrying back to Clover for cover when necessary."

She looked directly at Jason. "I thought Andy was in California at his new job."

"McCrae hasn't been to work in a couple of months," he told them. Phoebe shrugged, clearly still having trouble accepting that Andy McCrae was behind all the calls.

Lucas pulled her in tight. "It's almost over, baby."

"I know, but it is so strange to finally know who my stalker is. I need to call Corey and Shane."

Jason handed his cell to her. "Use mine."

All of Lucas's and his brothers' focus was on getting the fucker. Once the creep was dealt with, then they could move on to building a life together with Phoebe.

"I'll put him on speaker, in case he has some questions for you, Jason."

"Hello," Corey answered.

"Corey, it's Phoebe. Good news. The Wolfes have found out who my stalker is."

"I just found out, too. Andrew McCrae. I'm in my car and headed that way."

"Is Shane with you, Corey?" Phoebe's concern for Shane was never far from her thoughts.

"No. I tried to call him but he didn't answer."

Lucas saw Jason's face darken with frustration and Phoebe's tighten with worry. They were jumping the gun. Shane could be anywhere, but with Jason's ever by-the-book way of doing things and Phoebe's overwhelming sisterly love, Lucas understood why.

"You know our brother, sis." Corey's voice held all the years of frustration and worry that the entire Blue family had for Shane. "He's probably with some girl."

Corey's idea of where his brother might be didn't seem to change Phoebe's demeanor one bit. She was still concerned about Shane. Given all that had happened three years ago, Lucas, too, was worried. By the looks on Jason's and Mitchell's faces, he knew they felt the same way. But that was something to deal with later.

Right now, they had a stalker to take down. "Corey, how soon will you be here?"

"Almost there, I'm just around the corner. See you in sixty seconds."

The call ended.

"Once Corey gets here, me and my brothers will head to Clover, baby." Jason touched her cheek. She nodded. It was good to see that they'd gotten past the old hurts. "Not only is he your brother, but he is a US marshal, so I trust him to protect you."

"Me, too," Mitchell agreed. "If that fucker is there, he'll be sleeping and we can get the jump on him."

"Lucas and Mitchell, please raise your right hand," Jason instructed.

Mitchell's eyebrows rose up. "What for?"

"I need to deputize you both before we leave."

Lucas nodded. This was one time he was on board with Jason's by-the-book way of doing things.

Time to take down the motherfucker.

* * * *

Phoebe dialed Shane's number again. Still, no answer. "Where could he be, Corey?"

"You know how he is, sis." Corey sat next to her on the sofa.

She was so glad Corey was with her. He and Shane were the best brothers a girl could have. She never doubted they would do anything for her. But of the two, Corey was solid as a rock. Before the drug conviction, she would've sworn Shane was the same. "I'm worried sick about him and about the Wolfes."

"Of course you are." Corey grabbed her hand and squeezed. "Your guys will be fine. They know how to handle themselves."

"I still can't believe Andy McCrae is behind all the calls."

"Believe it or not, the evidence is very clear."

"Will he get jail time? He hasn't hurt me."

"Harassment is very serious, Phoebe, but the courts will have to decide what McCrae's penalty is. Maybe we should talk about something else."

"Small talk isn't going to help me relax. Not until they get back from Clover."

"It might not relax you, but maybe it could distract you," Corey said. "Speaking of the Wolfes, are you back together with all of them? It sure appears so."

Phoebe smiled. "We're better than we were, but we've still got so much to work out. You should've seen Jason's face when you said you couldn't get ahold of Shane. He automatically thinks the worst."

"Can you blame him, sis? It's going to take time for our brother to earn everyone's trust again, especially Jason's."

"How can he and I get past what happened with Shane? It's like a wedge between us that just won't go away."

"What Shane does is Shane's to deal with, Phoebe. You deserve happiness. Don't let our brother's mistakes drag you down. Jason loves you. So do Lucas and Mitchell. You four belong together. Mom and Dads know it. I know it. Hell, even Shane knows it."

A knock on the door made her jump to her feet.

"You expecting anyone?" he asked in a hushed tone.

"No." It was too soon for her three men to have returned from Clover.

"You stay here."

She nodded, feeling her heart pound hard in her chest. She grabbed her purse and pulled out her gun. Even though she wasn't defenseless, Phoebe was glad to have her big brother, a man who was a highly decorated former Marine and now a US marshal, with her.

"It might be Shane," she whispered as he got to his feet.

"Might be. Let me find out." Corey brought out his weapon. He peered through the peephole. "Nothing to worry about, sis." He holstered his gun. "It's only our parents."

"Did you tell them about my stalker?" She put Lady Equalizer away.

"Not me. I'm betting Shane did, though." He opened the door.

"Honey, are you okay?" Her mom ran to her side, taking a seat next to her on the sofa.

"I'm fine, Mom. What are you doing here?"

"You know exactly what we're doing here, young lady," Dad Curtis said in a tone that always sent a chill up and down her spine. "We're here because we heard about your stalker."

Dad Eddie shook his head. "Phoebe, you shouldn't have kept us in the dark about this. We're your family."

"I know, Dad, but you're dealing with so much already."

Her mom grabbed her hand. "Honey, we're your parents. We are supposed to take care of you, not the other way around."

"But I'm a grown woman, and with Shane just home from prison—"

"Stop right there. You always take on more than you should, but let us worry about Shane."

"Seems to me, sweetheart, you've been dealing with a ton of stuff yourself." Dad Curtis took a seat on the other side of Phoebe.

Dad Eddie put his arm around Corey's shoulder. "And what about you, young man. How long have you known about this stalker?"

"I swear, Dad, I just found out this morning."

Her mother sent Corey one of her famous disapproving looks. "We'll talk to you about that later."

Phoebe was puzzled. "How did you find out, anyway?"

"Shane," Dad Curtis answered. "He called the diner an hour ago.

We were there putting away the supplies from the catering van. He filled your mom in on everything."

Her mom let out a long, worried sigh. "No more secrets, baby. Promise me."

Seeing the concern in her parents' eyes crushed her. This was exactly why she had tried to keep the stalker issue from them. But now that they knew, she was glad to have them in her corner. They were the best parents in the world. "I was just trying to protect you, but okay, I promise."

"Do you know where Shane is?" Corey asked.

All three of their parents sighed.

Dad Eddie rolled his eyes. "He told Alice he was in Chicago."

"He's not allowed out of the county." Phoebe had read all the terms of Shane's parole. She shouldn't be surprised. Shane was the black sheep in the Blue family.

"Not without the sheriff's permission," Dad Curtis said. "Maybe Jason gave it to him."

"He was here just fifteen minutes ago," Corey informed them. "Jason had no idea where Shane was."

Their parents' faces fell.

Phoebe tried to contain her anxiety for her brother. Once again, Shane was running headfirst to trouble, dragging all of them down with him.

Her mother clasped her hands. "Where is the sheriff now?"

"Jason, Mitchell, and Lucas went to Clover." Her worry for her three men continued to roll through her.

Corey nodded. "Mom, Phoebe's stalker issue should be over tonight. Jason found out who the guy is. He and his brothers are headed to his house to arrest him."

She and Corey filled them in on all the details they'd learned about McCrae.

Dad Curtis put his arm around Phoebe. "Those boys will get that asshole."

Dad Eddied nodded. "The Wolfe brothers are good men, Phoebe."

"I'm worried about them," she confessed.

"Of course you are, baby. But everything is going to turn out fine. You'll see." Her mom kissed her on the cheek. " Since we're all up so late, would anyone like some coffee or wine?"

It was clear that her mom was trying to get all their minds off of what was happening in Clover.

"I wouldn't mind some wine, mom." She took a deep breath. "I've got something else I want to talk to you about."

"Forget the coffee. Let's all have some wine," Dad Curtis said. "It'll help us relax until the Wolfes return."

"I'll get it." Corey walked to the kitchen. "You visit with the folks."

"Okay, sweetheart. What is it you want to talk about?" her mom asked. "Perhaps I can help you. Does this have anything to do with you and the Wolfes? I did see you and Lucas sitting together at the O'Learys' Halloween party."

"I never can keep anything from you, Mom. And, yes, you're right. I want to talk to you about Jason, Mitchell, and Lucas."

"Oh, I'm so excited, dear. We've been waiting so long for a reconciliation."

Dad Curtis smiled. "This is the best news ever."

"I know it's been three years, but we gave them our permission for your hand." Dad Eddie grinned broadly. "We've never taken that back."

"Y'all are jumping the gun just a little bit." She looked at her parents and saw the unconditional love for her in their eyes. Growing up in their home had been wonderful. "It's true, but I have so much to work out, especially with Jason."

Her mom nodded. "Of the three, I can imagine you do with him."

"I still feel there's animosity between Shane and Jason. It worries me there will never be any trust between them. So, Mom, what do I do? I love them."

Corey returned carrying a tray with five glasses and an opened bottle of wine. "Did I miss anything?"

"Your sister was just telling us how she hooked up with the Wolfe brothers again," Dad Curtis said.

Phoebe's jaw dropped. "Dad?"

"What?" he said with a grin. "Oh, I forgot that means something else these days, doesn't it?"

"Yes, Dad, it does." She laughed and turned to Corey. "I was also telling them about how I was worried about Jason and asking them what they thought I should do."

Her mom took a sip of wine. "Honey, you know I never give advice unless you ask for it."

"Alice, you've got to be kidding." Dad Eddie laughed. "Ask...don't ask...you are always doling out advice like Chinese fortune cookies at Phong's Wok."

Her mom smiled at the two men she'd spent most of her life with. "With you two, I've had to. Neither of you would've proposed if I hadn't."

"What do you mean by that, baby?" Dad Curtis leaned forward and took her mom's hand, reaching over Phoebe's lap.

"I hinted and hinted, but neither of you figured out I was ready to say yes. Finally, when I told you the best place and time to propose was at midnight on Lover's Beach, you did."

Dad Eddie grabbed her mom's other hand. "And you made us the happiest men in the world, honey."

"Anyway, as I was saying before I was so rudely interrupted," her mom said, smiling. "The most important thing, Phoebe, is love. If you all love each other, everything else will work out. I promise you. I know Jason truly cares about Shane. When it comes to the men of Destiny, they can be a stubborn lot and Jason is one of the most headstrong and determined men in this town. Why do you think he was elected as sheriff? Because all of us knew he would never give up on anything. He would fight for us. And baby, he has proven again and again that he will fight for you, too. As a mom, I know there's more to the story about Shane than what we know. I know it in my heart."

"I want to believe that, Mom, but it's hard." The facts were clear and Shane was proving again, by breaking the terms of his probation, that he hadn't changed one bit. But in her heart, too, she still hoped Shane was the wonderful, loving, honest brother she'd always known.

"This whole situation is not your problem. It is between Shane and Jason. You love them both. Just keep it that way. Let them work this out."

"But mom, it's so hard to see two men that you love not care about one another."

"That's where you're wrong, sweetheart. They do care. They always have cared."

* * * *

With both his brothers by his side, Jason walked into the office of the motel.

"Hey, Sheriff," the man behind the counter said. "What brings you and your brothers out at this hour?"

"Ted, we've got a man, Andy McCrae, that I need to speak to."

"He checked in a couple of weeks ago. Paid a month in advance. Comes and goes as he pleases. What kind of trouble is he in?"

"I'll let you know after," Jason told him. "What room is McCrae in?"

"Now, Sheriff, you know I'm not supposed to tell you that without a warrant."

"How many years have you known me, Ted?"

"Since you were a kid."

"In all those years, have I ever steered you wrong?"

"Can't say that you have, Jason. And neither have Mitchell or Lucas."

"Okay then, I'm sure you don't want some hoodlum giving you trouble, running away your other customers. Right?"

"Sure thing, Sheriff. We may not be The Ritz, but I do try to run a tight ship."

"Let's have that number then."

"If you're sure it's okay?"

"I'm sure."

"It's room number twelve."

"Thanks Ted. You won't regret this."

The motel owner leaned back in his chair. "I hope you're right about that."

"I want you to sit tight, no matter what you hear, understand?"

"I'll be doing that, Sheriff."

"I need the key."

"Here it is, now be careful. Understand?" Ted said with a grin.

"Come on, bros, we've got some arresting to do."

With their guns drawn, Jason, Lucas, and Mitchell quietly approached room twelve. No lights were on.

"Looks like he's sleeping," Mitchell whispered, "which we'll help us get the drop on him."

"Lucas, go around back and make sure there's no escape route."

"Sure thing, bro," Lucas said quietly.

Jason stuck the key into the door, turning it very slowly, hoping not to disturb McCrae's sleep. Holding his breath, he waited for his eyes to adjust to the dark. The tiny room came into focus, though with dark patches of gray. A form was on the bed.

"Hands up, McCrae," Jason yelled and then he switched on the light.

The shape he'd seen in the bed turned out to be only pillows strewn across the mattress.

"He's not here, bro."

The door to the bathroom was ajar. Jason walked in and saw a gruesome scene. In the tub was a mutilated corpse, likely of Andy

McCrae.

"He's in here, Mitchell. Holler at Lucas to let him know."

Looking at the condition of the body, Jason scowled. *Not even this bastard deserved a death like this.*

Obviously, it had been slow and torturous. Fingers had been severed. Deep cuts were all over McCrae's body, including a large gash to his face. It looked as though death finally came by a stab wound to the heart.

When Lucas and Mitchell returned, he saw the look of horror on their faces.

"There's much more to this man than we know. I have some crime scene tape in my car to secure this area. I need to make sure no one enters until this is fully investigated. Will you take care of blocking off the scene while I make some calls?"

"We got this," Mitchell stated.

Jason walked away and called Brown, filling her in on all he'd discovered. Brown agreed with him that there was more to this than McCrae just being a stalker.

"Jason, I'll get a team out there right away to investigate. I know this is your jurisdiction, but I smell Lunceford in the middle of this. Do you agree?"

"Totally. I'll send my brothers to Phoebe. They'll let her know and make sure she's safe. I'll stay here until your team arrives." He didn't want to wait long. He wanted to get back to Phoebe as soon as possible. "Make sure they hurry."

"I will. Keep your ROC close by. I will contact you for follow-up."

Chapter Twelve

Phoebe jumped to her feet when Mitchell and Lucas walked in. "Oh my God, where's Jason? Is he okay?"

"He's fine, sweetheart." Lucas wrapped his arms around her. "Let's sit, and I'll tell you and your parents everything."

The intensity in his tone made her nervous. She sat down on the sofa and Lucas and Mitchell took a seat on either side of her.

"What happened in Clover, boys?" her mom asked.

Dad Eddie put his arm around her mother. "Did you find the bastard?"

Lucas's face darkened. "We did, Mr. Blue, but it didn't turn out the way we thought."

"Well, go on, boys," Dad Curtis urged. "Tell us everything."

She, Corey, and their parents listened intently to Lucas and Mitchell recount the horror they had found at the motel.

Andy McCrae is dead. Murdered. His body mutilated. "I just can't believe this."

"Honey, it's true." Mitchell put his arm around her and squeezed. "Every word."

"Being a stalker surely had nothing to do with McCrae getting killed." Corey's tone mirrored her thoughts. None of this added up. "There's more here than we know."

"Andy was strange, yes, but seemed so harmless." Phoebe recalled the awkward date she'd had with McCrae. Andy might've been a little weird, but he wasn't a killer and didn't deserve to die. "Why would anyone do such a thing? None of this makes any sense to me."

Lucas grabbed her hand. "I'm sure we'll know more once all the evidence is in."

"When will Jason be here?" Corey asked.

"As soon as the investigative team arrives," Mitchell answered, "he'll head this way."

* * * *

Standing in the motel room, Jason looked at his cell. The time kept ticking away. *Where are Brown's men?*

"Brought you a cup of coffee, Sheriff." Ted stood outside the open door.

The man clearly knew better than to cross the yellow tape.

He'd filled Ted in about how they'd found McCrae right before Lucas and Mitchell had left.

"Thanks, Ted, but you still can't come in here." He took the cup with his gloved hand. "It's a crime scene now. Murder. I'll stop by before I leave and clue you in on anything else that turns up."

"That'll be fine. I'll be in my office if you need anything."

He could tell the man was shaken.

He was anxious for Brown's team to arrive so he could leave and get back to Phoebe. He'd been standing since Lucas and Mitchell left, not wanting to taint the murder scene. He'd donned gloves and kept them on to make sure he didn't disturb any fingerprints or other evidence. He knew protocols and always followed them to the letter. The crime scene investigators were better trained at finding every shred of evidence in these kinds of cases. Best to leave it to the experts.

Once the agents arrived, he would give his statement and exit.

Sipping on the coffee, he glanced around the room one more time. Something on the floor caught his attention. He'd not seen it before because the comforter hid most of it. Carefully, he lifted the blanket and saw it was a billfold.

Is it McCrae's wallet or his killer's?

Phoebe's stalker was out of the picture. Who had killed McCrae and why? Would the murderer seek out Phoebe for some unknown reason?

Jason's gut tightened. He had to protect her. She was his responsibility. Always. "This is my jurisdiction," he told himself. Inside the leather of the wallet might be the answers he needed. Gently he grabbed the billfold by the corner, placing it on the bed.

He opened it, and what he saw shocked and crushed him. Going against all his training, against everything he believed—Jason placed the wallet in his pocket.

He knew who had killed McCrae.

His world and Phoebe's was about to be ripped apart again.

* * * *

Phoebe looked out the window and saw Jason drive up in his patrol car. "Thank God, he's here."

Corey jumped up and opened the door. Everyone was anxiously awaiting his arrival.

When Jason entered, they all started bombarding him with questions at once.

Jason held up his hands. "Just give me a second, I need a drink."

Phoebe could tell by his demeanor something was extremely wrong.

"What would you like, Jason?" her mom asked, always ready to help.

Her heart was thudding in her chest. "He drinks Jack Daniels straight up."

"Just sit down, Jason," Dad Eddie told him.

"Good idea," Dad Curtis said. "From what your brothers told us, I'm sure this was hard to digest."

"You don't know the half of it, Mr. Blue." Jason turned to

Mitchell and Lucas. "Did you tell them the condition we found McCrae's body in?"

"Yes," Lucas said. "We told them everything."

Jason's eyes landed on her. "All your family is here, Phoebe, but Shane. Where is he?"

Here we go again. "We don't know," she answered truthfully.

He took the glass from her mom and drained it dry in one gulp.

"Jason, you know Shane." Corey's tone was filled with concern. "He's likely holed up at some woman's house."

Her mom poured Jason another shot.

He drank it. "Shane better still be in town."

Phoebe tensed, not liking where this conversation was going. "Leaving would be against the terms of his parole. I'm certain he's still here."

"I'm not," Jason stated flatly.

"What in the hell does this have to do with what happened in Clover?" Lucas stood and folded his arms over his chest. The old animosity between him and Jason seemed to have returned in a flash.

Mitchell stepped next to Lucas, staring down at Jason. "Can't you drop your übercop attitude when it comes to Shane for tonight and tell us about McCrae's murder instead?"

"That's what I'm trying to do. Shane's in trouble."

Her heart seized in her chest. "What do you mean by that?"

Jason's face fell.

"Tell me," she demanded. "Don't hold back." *Not again, Jason. Please. Open up and tell me.*

"I have reason to believe he killed McCrae."

Her mom shook her head defiantly. "I don't care what you found or how bad it looks. I know my son just as well as I know you, Jason Christopher Wolfe. Shane is no murderer. You know it and I know it."

"I want to believe that, Alice. I do."

Phoebe couldn't wrap her head around what Jason was saying.

She felt the old hurt bubble up like acid in her throat. "Why would you say such a thing? We just got Shane back."

He didn't answer, but his stare never left her.

Corey's face darkened. "What makes you think my brother is responsible, Jason? What evidence do you have?"

"I can't say, but he's in trouble. I'll do everything I can to help."

"Like you did before," she snapped back. "Don't do this family any favors, Sheriff. You can go. Now."

Jason looked resigned to saying good-bye again. "I'm sorry about this. I truly am."

"Sorry?" All the feelings she'd had when he'd sent Shane away to prison began stinging once again, but this time with even more pain. "I don't believe you, Jason. Not one damn bit. You've been gunning for Shane since he got back in town. You say you think he's responsible somehow for what happened to Andy but you won't tell us why. Well, mister, I'm a lawyer. I will use everything in my power to make sure he doesn't go back."

"I'm sure you will," he said quietly.

Why is he doing this again?

"This doesn't make any sense," Lucas jumped in, his voice laden with hot irritation. "We only found out about Andy's location from Brown. How would Shane have found out before us, Sheriff?"

The old bitterness between the brothers was back in full force.

Jason shrugged. "He was in the pen for three years. I'm sure he made some pretty sketchy friends."

"So? What does that mean?" Mitchell's face thundered with rage.

"What your brother is suggesting is criminals get intel much faster than law enforcement," Corey answered. "Even if that's true, Jason, I still can't believe Shane would go alone. He would've called me first. Mom is right. My brother is no killer."

"I hope you're right," Jason said. "But McCrae was stalking Phoebe. I could see myself putting a bullet through the son of a bitch for your sister. I can understand how your brother could do the same."

"Just stop. Nothing you can say will change how I feel about you right now. Did you not hear me, Sheriff? I told you to go." Her heart was being ripped to shreds. She was on the verge of tears, but she would be damned if she shed a single drop in front of Jason. "This is my house and unless you have a warrant, leave."

"Until McCrae's murderer is brought in, whether that turns out to be your brother or not, you need protection, Phoebe."

"I can handle things myself. Get out."

"Honey, calm down." Her mom's gentle gaze locked in on her. "Jason said he's going to do everything he can to help Shane, and right now, we need everyone. I believe Jason will help us."

"Mom, please. Don't." Arguing with her mother was a no-win endeavor. "We'll talk about this later."

"Jason, let's go to your office." Corey obviously wanted to know more. "I bet together we can work this out. There's a real killer on the loose, and you and I have the skills to flush out the bastard."

Jason's stare never left Phoebe. "I would appreciate your help, Corey."

She loved him with all her heart, but what he'd said about Shane, what he suspected of him, what he was willing to do to her brother, tore her apart. She was so confused.

Say something, Phoebe. Don't let him walk out again. Not again. But her lips remained sealed. She was apparently destined to repeat the past.

Jason took a deep breath and his eyes left hers. He exited without another word.

"Sis, don't worry." Corey gave her a hug. "We'll get this cleared up."

"Shane is a lot of things, but he's no murderer. Your dads and I will see if we can find him." Her mom turned to Mitchell and Lucas. "Will you two stay with Phoebe tonight?

"Mom, I'm fine."

"You heard your brother, Phoebe. There's a killer on the loose.

No way am I leaving you alone. Either the Wolfes stay with you or we are taking you home with us."

"We'll be happy to stay with Phoebe, Mrs. Blue," Lucas said.

Mitchell nodded. "She'll be safe with us."

Phoebe's hands were curled into fists. She'd just let Jason walk out the door and hadn't made a single move to stop him.

Why does he always have to act like an ass?

Obviously Jason was shaken. Why? Did he still care for Shane? *What damn evidence does he think he has? Doesn't matter. He's wrong about everything.*

Her world was falling apart. She needed Lucas and Mitchell to hold her, to tell her everything was going to be okay.

"Are you fine with this plan, baby girl?" Dad Curtis put his hand on her shoulder. "Staying with Mitchell and Lucas? If not, you can go home with us."

"Yes, Daddy. I want to stay."

* * * *

Jason sat behind his desk, hating everything about the job he'd worked so hard to get. In his pocket was Shane's wallet, the thing that would put his old friend away for a very long time.

"It's just us lawmen now. So, what evidence do you have that makes you think Shane killed McCrae?" Corey asked flatly.

"Too soon to reveal that to you."

"Really?" Corey frowned. "Something is up with you."

"I'm not sure what you mean." *I know this can't have been Shane. God, why did I rush to Phoebe and say Shane was a murderer?*

"Don't bullshit me, Jason. I've known you my whole life. You're holding back and not because of some legal protocol."

"I fucked up, Corey. Fucked up bad once again." He'd kept what had happened at the diner three years ago to himself. A heavy burden he'd carried for Phoebe to protect her from the darkness Shane had rushed into of his own free will. But this new hell was too much to bear alone.

"Talk to me, Jason. I know you care about Shane as much as I do. This sucks, but you know more than you're telling me."

I have to trust someone, don't I? "If I do tell you, it could mean my job, my badge, and possibly my freedom. I could go to prison." He took a deep breath and reached into his pocket and touched Shane's wallet. "You're a fucking US marshal."

"And you're a damn sheriff. Come on, buddy. I've got your back."

He placed the billfold on his desk. "This is Shane's. I found it at the motel where McCrae was killed."

Corey's eyebrows shot up, realizing what this piece of evidence meant for Shane. "Why in the hell do you have this?"

"I knew Shane would be arrested and sent back to prison with this kind of evidence. I can understand why Shane would've wanted to kill the motherfucker. Hell, we all wanted to. All the way from the motel to Phoebe's house I kept thinking how I would've done the same thing. I tried to hold back from your family, from Phoebe, but I just couldn't. Not again. I wish I had kept my mouth shut. I think I was wrong to accuse Shane. Corey, McCrae's body was mutilated. That's not something your brother would've done."

"Unless he was high on drugs at the time," Corey added, his face dark with concern.

"Maybe. But you should've seen it. Gruesome. I just can't figure it out. So, I took the billfold."

"You can't blame yourself, Jason. You were shaken. Taking evidence from a crime scene is against everything you believe in. It's not like you at all. You wanted to be honest with my sister and my whole family and not make the same mistake you did before." Corey sighed. "It's wrong to have removed the billfold, Jason, but I would've done the same damn thing. He's my brother. Now, we've got our work cut out for us because we've got to get to the bottom of this."

Jason nodded. "I'm glad you and I are on the same page."

"If Shane did do this, we need to find him before the investigators figure out he was there. I'm sure his wallet wasn't the only evidence left. They'll find something else that will put him at the scene. If he comes forward and confesses, it should help get him a lighter sentence. Killing McCrae, his sister's stalker, should be considered a crime of passion."

"That's a whole bunch of *ifs*, Corey. I still don't think Shane did this. He's capable of a lot. We both know that. But not this. It just doesn't make sense."

"Whatever it turns out to be, Jason, you and I will work together. Like I said before. I've got your back."

"Same here. And we both need to have Shane's back, too." Jason hoped they could save Shane from whatever demons he faced, whether they were on the inside or outside. *Before it is too late.*

Chapter Thirteen

Mitchell handed a glass of wine to Phoebe. He and Lucas each held a beer. "We all need to take a second, probably several, to clear our heads about what we just learned from Jason."

"What exactly did we learn?" Lucas snapped back. "Nothing. Jason thinks Shane murdered McCrae, but as usual, he didn't give us any real details as to why."

"I don't think my head will ever be clear again." She stared at the wine glass in her hand. "This couldn't be more horrible."

"Baby, we can work this all out." Mitchell hated seeing the pain in her eyes. "Together."

"Mitchell, you're wrong." She looked at him. "We are not together. Not really."

Knowing how sad and frustrated she felt was killing him and ripping him to shreds. "Don't say that, sweetheart."

"Mitchell, I screwed up letting you in again." She turned to Lucas. "You, too. And Jason. We shouldn't have tried to rekindle our flame. We're repeating the same mistakes all over again."

Hearing the suffering in her voice was gut wrenching. "The only one who screwed up was Jason. Not you. Not me. Not Lucas."

"It doesn't matter. My heart is breaking apart again. I thought we could go back to the way it was before Shane, but now I know we can never go back. Shane will always be a wedge between us."

"He's not to me. Shane's not capable of the horror we saw at the motel." He grabbed her hand. "Jason is wrong, Phoebe. Whatever we need to do to make sure your brother stays out of prison, I'm on board."

She pulled her hand away. "So you think he did it? You think he killed McCrae?"

"Honey, I didn't say that," he said as gently as he could. "I just said that whatever we need to do to keep him out of prison, that's what we need to do."

"Baby, you're the attorney here." Lucas's tone was soft. He, too, knew how fragile she was right now. "You know how to navigate the justice system better than anyone I know. Tell us what to do."

She sighed. "I'm not sure having you help me save Shane is a good idea, guys. You're Jason's brother. Shane is mine."

They were treading on thin ice. Phoebe was ready to end everything again. Who could blame her after Jason's pronouncement, followed by his refusal to say why he believed Shane had committed the murder.

"Honey, I would've killed McCrae for the shit he put you through." For her protection, Mitchell knew he would go to whatever lengths necessary. She was the love of his life and he wouldn't allow anyone to harm her. "I don't think Shane took the fucker out, but I certainly can understand why he would want to."

"Maybe so, but would you have mutilated Andy's body? That's what you told me and my parents you saw."

"No. Of course not." He knew she had a point. Killing someone to protect the one you love was one thing. Mutilation was another. "That's why I know Shane didn't do this."

Phoebe let out a long breath. "I'm glad you agree with me."

"So do I, baby," Lucas confessed.

"I wish Jason felt the same way." Phoebe closed her eyes. "I really need to be alone right now. It's obvious that everyone, including my mom, wants me to have bodyguards. Fine. You can stay. One of you can take the guest bedroom. The other can take the couch. I have to pack. Ashley and I are leaving for Chicago in the morning. I wish I could I get out of it, but I have no choice. Jennifer is depending on me."

"Why?" Lucas asked.

"If you must know, I have a deposition to conduct for the case I'm working on for Jennifer. It's scheduled for the first thing Monday morning."

"I heard about that," he said. "Braxton Meat Packing is suing her ranch for selling them diseased cattle, right?"

He knew that Lucas was just trying to keep Phoebe talking, to keep her from shutting them out. In the past, talking about the law or her cases always kept her engaged. He hoped it would now."

She sat down her wine glass and stood. "Good night."

Without another word, she marched into her bedroom, shutting the door.

He and Lucas stared at the closed door for a long moment.

"What a fucking mess, Mitchell." Lucas downed the rest of his beer and headed back into the kitchen. "Another beer?"

"Absolutely."

Lucas handed him his drink. "I really wanted to help her, but what could we do? Jason fucked up everything once again."

"We will help her. She just needs time alone, which is understandable given all that went down tonight."

Lucas sat down and they drank their beers in silence for a bit. "We've got to go to Chicago with her."

"I know. She's not going to be happy about that."

"Not one damn bit. Our girl has fire."

"Like a bonfire." He loved her. Somehow they would get through this nightmare. They had to. "I can't lose her, Lucas. I won't. Not again. Not ever."

"Me either. Fuck. Why is Jason doing this again? After three years, we finally have her in our arms."

Mitchell shook his head. "I hate to say this, bro, but if Jason doesn't fix things between him and Phoebe, I intend to move on with her—with or without him."

Lucas sighed. "Me, too. Damn, I never dreamed I would consider a life, a family, without Jason. Even after the breakup and dealing with all the anger that unearthed inside me, I still thought eventually that you, Jason, and me would share Phoebe once again. That we would build a future together."

Mitchell had been sure they were going to make it. He still was. "So did I, bro. And even with all the shit he unloaded tonight, I still haven't given up."

Lucas took a sip of his beer. "I haven't either, but you have to admit the chances for that happening are shrinking."

"You saw Jason's face tonight." Mitchell could tell that Jason had really struggled with what to do. "There's more to the story than he shared. I have to believe he will come around soon, but for now, I will do whatever I have to do to keep Phoebe."

"Same here."

They finished their beers in silence.

"We need some clothes for the trip, Mitchell."

Lucas was right. There was a lot to do before leaving in the morning. "I'll go to my place and pack a few things. You stay here with her."

Lucas handed him the keys to his place. "You mind getting my bag packed?"

"Sure. Kill two birds with one stone."

"I'll call Ashley to find out what flight they're booked on," Lucas said. "Then I'll check with the airline to see if there are at least two seats available. If not, I'll call the Knights to see if we can use their jet tomorrow."

"That covers all the bases for now."

"All of them, but one." Lucas frowned. "We still need to find Shane."

"Corey is shadowing Jason." Mitchell walked to the door. "I'll text him to see what they've learned so far."

"One step at a time, bro."

"That's all we can do." He left Phoebe's house, praying for a miracle.

* * * *

Just before four in the morning, Jason stood next to Corey in front of the Blues' home. They'd been working all night, trying to locate Shane. They'd engaged Brown, hoping to use her vast resources at the CIA to find Shane. Nothing so far, but each of them held the ROCs she'd given the entire team, hoping to hear from her soon.

Going through Shane's room for any clue that might tip them off to his location was a last ditch effort.

Jason was losing hope and fast. He couldn't get the image of how Phoebe looked at him when he'd told her that he thought Shane had killed McCrae.

I've lost her for good. She was his world and he'd destroyed every chance they had.

Corey had gotten a text from Mitchell earlier, asking if they'd found Shane and what was going on with the investigation. He'd called him back and found out that Phoebe was headed to Chicago in the morning with Ashley and that Lucas and Mitchell were going with them. *Phoebe might as well be headed to the other side of the moon when it comes to me. My brothers, too.* Things were about to return to the way they'd been for the last three years. He couldn't bear the loneliness. Not again. *Why didn't I just keep my mouth shut?* Because she'd asked him to be honest with her. She deserved that from him, after everything that happened between them. *Still, I could've tossed Shane's wallet into the lake and been done with it.*

"My parents' bedroom is in the very back of the house," Corey said. "If we keep quiet, I'm sure we won't disturb them."

Jason hadn't been inside the home since the breakup with Phoebe, but he still remembered how it was laid out. Phoebe's teenage bedroom was next to Shane's, but she hadn't lived there in years. When Shane had returned from prison, it was the stipulation of the parole board that he live with his parents during his probation.

Corey unlocked the door. They walked inside. The place was dark and quiet.

When they got to Shane's room, they went in and shut the door behind them.

Corey went to the closet and he headed to the chest of drawers. They hoped to find something, anything, that would help them find him.

Jason scanned the items on top of Shane's dresser. Seeing the picture of him and Shane when they were teenagers brought back so many memories. Holding up a string of fish they'd caught that day, their arms were around each other's shoulder. He remembered it like it was yesterday.

What happened to you, Shane?

They'd been so close. Like brothers. How he wished it could be again.

Shane had kept the picture and framed it. That puzzled Jason. *Why?* After what had gone down in the diner between them, he found it hard to understand.

He glanced around the room and saw only one other picture, this one of the entire Blue family. He turned back to the photo of the two of them. *I sent you to prison, Shane. You should hate me. I know I hate myself for it.*

"Anything?" Corey asked quietly.

"Not yet." He saw the light on his ROC blink. The ID let him know it was Agent Brown. "This is Brown," he told Corey.

He clicked it on and an image of Joanne Brown's face appeared.

"Wolfe here. So is Marshal Blue."

"Guys, I've got a tip about your missing man. Looks like he's in Chicago."

Jason's gut tightened. "You have an address."

"I might have one that will help you, but you're not going to like it. Take a look at this picture. It was taken today by an agent. It'll explain plenty."

Seeing the photo on the screen confirmed his worst nightmares.

Shane was walking next to Niklaus Mitrofanov, along with other Russian mobsters. "Fuck."

The marshal's face darkened in shock. "Brown, we need an address."

Jason was beginning to believe that his old friend might've been capable of killing McCrae.

"All I can give you is the place we believe Mitrofanov runs his operation from. It's a warehouse in South Side. We've got intel that he plans on turning the five million in diamonds over to the Chicago mafia day after tomorrow. He's trying to save his neck. I've already got a man on the ground there. Remember, Jason, our focus isn't on Mitrofanov or The Outfit. We're still trying to flush out Lunceford."

"I agree, but I need to bring in Niklaus. I'm still sheriff." *But for how long?* The photo painted a clear picture. Shane was running with the Russian mafia, and his wallet was still in Jason's pocket. *I tampered with evidence.* "Mitrofanov is enemy number one in Destiny, Brown. That's got to be my main focus for now."

"I know you and Corey want to apprehend both Niklaus and Shane. I thought you would feel this way, so I worked it out with Dylan. The TBK jet is ready to take you to Chicago."

Corey's concern for both his brother and sister was evident by the look on his face. "There might be an issue, Brown."

"Jason's brothers are trying to get on a commercial flight in the morning with my sister and her assistant. They're also going to Chicago. If they can't get seats, I'm sure they will call Scott and Eric."

Brown shook her head. "No one can know you're going."

"Agreed." Jason wanted to keep Phoebe from being hurt. Yes, she would eventually learn that Shane had screwed up even more than any of them had imagined possible. But not now. Not tonight.

"Why are they going to Chicago?" Brown asked.

Corey told her about Phoebe's deposition on Monday and why Lucas and Mitchell needed to accompany her and Ashley.

"No problem," Brown said. "I'll make sure Jason's brothers can get seats."

Jason wasn't surprised she could get something like that done. Agent Brown was capable of a lot of things.

"You're walking into a hornets' nest, guys, but if you can take down Mitrofanov before the exchange and retrieve the diamonds, we might be able to use that to our advantage to trap Lunceford. We recorded a call from Lunceford to Mitrofanov a couple of hours ago. Needless to say, they aren't friends anymore. Lunceford told Mitrofanov that he better turn the diamonds over to him or there would be hell to pay."

"Now Niklaus has two hits out on him," Corey said.

He nodded. "The bastard will be lucky if he makes it out alive."

"Lunceford believes he is owed the five million since he orchestrated the whole con against TBK. The call originated from an apartment in St. Louis. With MacCabe, Jena, and Dixon on their honeymoon, that leaves us three agents short. Dylan and I are headed there now. I'll put you in touch with my man in Chicago. Keep your ROCs with you, gentlemen, so we can communicate with each from both operational sites. With the level of security we have, Lunceford cannot break into them. We don't want him tipped off that we are coming."

After a few other details were worked out, they ended the call.

Jason had a really bad feeling about this trip. "I know Brown said she would make sure my brothers can get tickets, but I'm thinking we should pull the plug on Phoebe's trip to Chicago completely. Shane is there. Mitrofanov, too."

"It's a big city, Jason," Corey said. "It's an unfortunate coincidence that my sister is going there the same time we are, but she always stays on the Miracle Mile whenever she's in Chicago. She'll be miles away from the South Side."

Jason glanced at the photo of him and Shane one more time before leaving with Corey for the airport.

Chapter Fourteen

Phoebe placed her briefcase on the conference table. "Where are the Braxton people?"

"They should've been here by now," Ashley informed. "As of yesterday, they confirmed they would be here."

"Get them on the phone. Find out what the delay is."

"Will do, boss."

As Ashley made the call, Phoebe took a seat. Her mind wasn't really on the Steele case. All she could think about was what Jason suspected about Shane. Murder. Not possible. Her whole world was crumbling and she wasn't sure there was anything she could do about it. She loved Jason. She loved Mitchell and Lucas, too. But she also loved her brother.

She turned to the floor-to-ceiling glass wall and gazed at two of the three men she wished she could spend the rest of her life with. Mitchell and Lucas sat together, scanning every person who walked by, clearly making sure none posed a threat. They were on high alert for her. Silly, since no one was gunning for her now. Andy McCrae was dead. The only threat now was to her heart.

"The Braxton team is on their way now, Phoebe."

She took in a deep breath, hoping to clear her thoughts. She had a job to do. Jennifer Steele was not only her friend, but also her client in this case. Whatever was happening in Phoebe's personal life must be put aside for the next few hours.

Three men appeared on the other side of the glass. Mitchell and Lucas stood up and said something to them.

She waved at her self-appointed bodyguards to let the men pass.

The Wolfe brothers didn't budge. Clearly, Mitchell and Lucas weren't going to let the men into the room until they were satisfied the trio from Braxton was harmless. She saw one of the men reach into his jacket and pull out an identification card.

For a brief moment, she smiled. But it vanished just as quickly when she thought about how hard it was going to be to say good-bye again. Mitchell and Lucas hadn't told her that they were willing to be with her without Jason, should that become necessary, but she sensed they would.

Not possible. *I love them all. I won't separate them.*

Being with Mitchell and Lucas now, in Chicago, was crushing her. There was a void, an absence that kept pounding at the back of her mind. *Jason.* Trying to build a life with one or two of the brothers would only end in heartbreak. Each was unique and wonderful, but all three were connected and reminded her of the others.

Finally, Mitchell and Lucas seemed satisfied, allowing the trio of Braxton men to come into the conference room.

"Hello, Ms. Blue." The tallest of the three, and clearly the leader, held out his hand.

She took it. "You must be Mr. Jenkins."

"Yes, I am. Nice to finally put a face to a name."

"It is. This is my assistant, Ashley Vaughn."

"These are my associates, Nicholas Walker and Sylas Hayes."

Someone was missing. She'd come to talk to the company's vet, not these people. "And where is Harrison Rutledge? He's the one I'm deposing."

Jenkins's face tightened. "Mr. Rutledge will not be coming today, counselor."

She'd come all the way to Chicago to talk to the man. What were they trying to pull? "Then why am I here, sir?"

"Please sit, Ms. Blue. There's been a change you need to hear."

"Five minutes, Mr. Jenkins. Please don't waste any more of my time."

"I won't."

They all took their seats.

"Braxton is withdrawing their case against your client," Jenkins began. "Harrison Rutledge is no longer with the company. Mr. Walker and Mr. Hayes discovered several discrepancies in the records on file."

Phoebe had, too, but was saving that information if the case made it to trial.

Jenkins turned to the two younger men. "Give me the file, please."

Both his associates were quite handsome and were having quite an impact on Ashley, who couldn't seem to keep her eyes off of them.

Mr. Jenkins pushed a file in front of her, its contents the official withdrawal of the case. "This whole thing was a mix-up."

"More than that, I'm certain. My client will be relieved to hear Braxton is dropping the case. I know Mrs. Steele well. She will not take Braxton back to court to seek compensation for any kind of damages, I can assure you. Off the record, what else did you find?"

Jenkins studied her for a moment before turning to the other men. "Tell her what you uncovered."

"We found that Mr. Harrison Rutledge was a total fraud," Walker said. "He came to Braxton a year ago with a resume containing credentials a mile long, all of them false."

"Didn't your HR department verify the information on his resume?" She couldn't wait to let Jennifer know they'd won, but even more she wanted to get back to Destiny and back to trying to find Shane.

"They did," Hayes said. "That's what's so strange about this. When we got to digging after we suspected Rutledge had falsified the records, we rechecked everything, hoping to find something that would lead us to a connection to why he would do such a thing. Every place we contacted—his university, prior employees, prior residences, even his credit history—was blank. It was as if he never existed."

"I don't understand. How would he benefit if Braxton won a case against Steele?" Ashley asked.

Jenkins answered, "He wouldn't have. That's what is so very strange. He wouldn't have gotten one red cent. There's got to be more to this than we know at this point."

Walker shook his head. "Rutledge has vanished into thin air, but we do have the police trying to locate him and our own personal detectives."

Phoebe wondered what the guy's motive had been. "Will you keep me informed if you find out anything?"

"Certainly, Ms. Blue." Jenkins leaned forward in his chair. "I just want you to know that Braxton is a very reputable company and we intend to pay all of your expenses, plus pay for all the hours that you put into this case."

"That's very kind of you, Mr. Jenkins. After my investigation, I knew your company was very prestigious. I also have known Mrs. Steele for many years and knew how credible she is. That's why none of this case made any sense to me."

"I'm glad we could clear this all up before going to trial."

"You know we would have won." Phoebe grinned and stood, offering her hand.

"I know your reputation, too." He shook her hand. "Like I said, I'm very glad we didn't have to face you in court. It would've been quite the battle."

Walker and Hayes rose, each shaking her hand. They turned their attention back to Ashley. They held Ashley's hand a little longer than was proper etiquette. Phoebe could see that there was definitely chemistry between Ashley and the two men.

After Jenkins and his two associates left, Lucas and Mitchell entered the conference room.

"Ready to head back to Destiny?" Mitchell asked.

Ashley smiled. "Not before shopping and some dinner. Our flight doesn't leave until ten tonight. Sitting at O'Hare for hours isn't my idea of a good time. Besides, Phoebe and I have a tradition of visiting the Magnificent Mile whenever we are in Chicago. I think she could use the distraction, don't you two?"

"I'm not sure I'm up for shopping, Ash." Actually, she knew she wasn't. She hated that their flight was so late in the day. "I could certainly use something to eat."

Hayes stepped back into the conference room. "Excuse me. Might I borrow Ms. Vaughn for a moment?"

Phoebe smiled, seeing the light in the man's blue eyes. "Certainly."

Ash's cheeks brightened to a lovely shade of pink. She followed him out into the lobby.

Mitchell grinned. "Looks like there might be a love connection happening."

Suddenly, Walker returned, nearly shoving Hayes to the side, jealousy written all over his face.

"Oh boy," Lucas said. "We might have trouble brewing instead."

She and the Wolfes had grown up in Destiny, a place where poly families were the norm. It was hard for them to understand why love didn't work that way for everyone.

She sighed. *What am I thinking? Nothing about love is working for me. It's a complete fucked-up mess.*

Ashley walked back into the conference room. "They want to take me to dinner at that French restaurant just across the street, Phoebe."

Mitchell's eyebrows shot up. "Both of them? Together?"

"Not at first," Ash admitted. "I told them that I would only go if I didn't have to choose between them."

"Good for you." Phoebe remembered Ash telling her about the struggle she'd had with three men back in her hometown in Nevada. "Go. Have fun."

"But, boss, they're not from Destiny."

"It's only a date. Relax." She put her arm around Ash. "Go to dinner with them. That's an order."

"Aye-aye, sir." Ash laughed. She left with the Braxton men.

"You said you could eat," Mitchell said. "Me, too. What are you hungry for?"

Before she could answer, a text came in on her cell.

* * * *

The morning sun was hidden behind dark clouds. A storm was coming.

The South Side Chicago neighborhood looked like a war zone. The glory days of the two-story houses lining Blackwell Avenue had clearly gone by long ago. Most windows and doors were boarded up. Piles of litter could be seen in every direction.

Jason and Corey remained in the car with Neil Smith, the CIA agent Brown had sent them to. They were all taking stock of the impoverished place.

Three men leaned against a tree that was in dire need of trimming. Several teenage boys on skateboards went up and down the street.

"Something is off about this," Corey said.

He nodded, feeling the same. "Doesn't look like that place has any occupants at all to me." Glancing down at his ROC one more time, he verified the address. The white house in the middle of the block was the one Brown had told them was Mitrofanov's headquarters of operation.

"I agree." Smith seemed like a typical CIA spook, secretive and dedicated. "This is too far from the action the Russian is into. Mitrofanov's son, Sergei, ran drugs through an orphanage ten miles from here, but that was shut down a while back after your people took him out in Destiny."

The Stone brothers had rescued Amber from Sergei Mitrofanov. That had started the ball rolling. Niklaus wanted revenge against the entire town for the loss of his son.

Corey opened the car door. "Let's get to it."

Jason admired Corey's determination. Shane was in trouble,

mixed up with Niklaus Mitrofanov somehow and likely the killer of McCrae. They needed to find Shane and soon.

They walked up to the door, each holding their weapons.

The kids in the street stopped skating and the men by the tree stopped passing the bottle.

They seemed to know something was about to go down.

Maybe they were wrong about the house being abandoned.

* * * *

Phoebe looked at the text on her cell and felt her heart jump up into her throat. It was from Shane.

Sis, I need you. I heard you were in Chicago. So am I. I'm sorry for all the pain I've put you through. Please come and get me. I'm at 11368 South Mainstee Road.
Love,
Shane

"What's wrong, baby?" Mitchell asked.

She handed him her phone. "We've got to go. Now."

Mitchell read the text. "She got a message from Shane." He handed the phone to Lucas.

Her pulse raced. "I've got to help my brother."

Lucas put his arm around her. "Try to call him, baby."

Mitchell nodded. "Great idea, bro."

"Yes, it is." She took the phone from Lucas and clicked on Shane's number. "It went straight to voice mail. That's not unusual for him. He always forgets to charge his phone."

"Phoebe, call Corey and let him know about the text," Mitchell said.

"No. He's working with Jason" She stood, feeling every beat of her heart in her temples. "I want to wait until we hear Shane's side of the story."

Lucas nodded. "Let's get a cab and go get him."

As they rushed out of the conference room together, she felt anxious and said a silent prayer.

Let Shane be innocent.

* * * *

Jason shoved the door to the house on Blackwell Avenue open.

He, Corey, and Agent Smith rushed in fully armed.

What they found crushed his hope for Shane. The place looked abandoned.

"This is a fucking dead end." Corey's face filled with worry for his brother.

"The cameras in every corner tell me that this was the property of someone pretty paranoid," Smith said.

Jason agreed. "Probably Mitrofanov. His home in Destiny had a ton of surveillance equipment."

"I read the report on that." Smith handed him and Corey rubber gloves. "It blew up with one of the Agency's best inside, didn't it?"

"Agent Black." Jason remembered the explosion. "He was a good man."

"Fuck. This doesn't help me one damn bit. I need to find my brother." Corey holstered his gun and pulled out his ROC. "I'm contacting Brown."

"Hold on." Jason pointed to the only thing in the space—a metal folding chair near the back wall. "There's something in the seat."

"A bomb?" Smith kept his gun in his hand.

Jason took a step closer. "Looks like a laptop. There's an ashtray on the floor, too." It was filled with cigarette butts. He bent down. "They all have red lipstick on them."

"Who the hell is the woman?" Corey stepped forward, likely to get a closer look.

"Mitrofanov doesn't have a woman working for him," Smith informed. "This is very strange."

Jason opened the laptop and what he saw shocked him to his very core.

An image of Shane appeared on the screen. He was sitting in a chair, his hands behind his back and a gun to his head.

The man holding the gun was none other than Niklaus Mitrofanov.

"Motherfucker." Corey was clearly unable to contain his rage.

Under the photo was an arrow with the word *More*.

Jason clicked on it and a text message filled the screen.

Gentlemen,

As you can see, I have Shane Blue in my custody. I understand you care for him deeply. Having lost my son and nephews to tragic endings, I know how you must feel seeing him in such dire straits. Unlike what I received from you and your little town, I offer you a chance to change his circumstances.

I want to negotiate with you, Sheriff Wolfe. I'm sure we can come to an agreement that will benefit us both.

I calculate your driving time to be at an hour to get to my location. Be here in fifty or poor Shane will not be among us anymore.

Come directly to 11368 South Mainstee Road. Come now.

Sincerely,

Niklaus Mitrofanov

Chapter Fifteen

Phoebe stared at the warehouse on Mainstee Road. The building was run-down and every wall filled with graffiti. "God, what is Shane doing here?"

Mitchell put his arm protectively around her. "Let's go inside and find out, baby."

They walked up the steps to the door. When it opened, it creaked loudly, adding to her anxiety.

They stepped into an empty room, twenty feet by twenty feet, loaded with boxes. The door directly in front of them was made of steel. There was a keypad next to it. What was on the other side?

She took a deep breath. "Shane, where are you? It's Phoebe. I'm here."

Without warning, she was grabbed from behind with a gun piercing her back. Mitchell and Lucas, their eyes full of shock and rage, had suffered the same fate.

From the steel door, two more men with guns appeared. The massive door closed with a loud clang, followed by several metallic sounds. It looked and sounded impenetrable.

Outnumbered and outgunned.

She, Lucas, and Mitchell had flown to Chicago the day before, so they had to leave their weapons behind. God, how she wished she had Lady Equalizer right now. It likely wouldn't have made any difference in this situation, since the bastards had gotten the drop on them, but it certainly would've made her feel better.

"I haven't had the pleasure of meeting you before," one of the two men in front of them said with a Russian accent. "I apologize for the reception of my father's men. This is a very dangerous neighborhood. We take security very seriously." He smiled, and she felt a chill run up and down her spine. "Let me introduce myself. I'm Roman Mitrofanov. You are?"

This guy is Niklaus's son. "Cut the crap. You know exactly who I am, mister," she said, pulling courage from some secret place inside her, overcoming her fear. *Shane needs me.* "I am here to get my brother, Shane."

"Shane Blue is your brother?"

"You know he is," she answered.

Was Roman just toying with her or did he really not know?

Out of the corner of her eye, she could see Lucas and Mitchell. Two of the thugs, the biggest ones of the lot, held her guys by the necks with guns at their backs.

Lucas and Mitchell clearly hadn't given up, as the determination on their faces revealed they were looking for an opportunity to make an escape.

"That means you must be Phoebe Blue, since Shane only has one sister. Pleasure to meet you. Who are your gentlemen friends, Ms. Blue?"

"You harm one hair on her head, asshole, and I swear I will kill you," Mitchell choked out.

Roman smiled. "Sir, I don't believe you are in any position to make threats. Besides, I only want to know who you are. We don't have many drop-in guests."

The guy next to Roman stepped forward and punched Mitchell in the gut. "Answer him."

She had to stop this before someone got hurt. "His name is Mitchell Wolfe."

Roman's jaw dropped. "One of the sheriff's brothers?" He turned his evil gaze to Lucas. "You must be the other brother."

Her heart pounded violently in her chest. "We didn't come here to make trouble. I only want to find my brother and we will leave. I swear."

"There seems to have been some sort of mistake, Roman," the man holding her said. "Your brother would know what to do about this situation."

"Anton is not here," Roman said in a growl. "I am. Now, shut up and let me think."

Phoebe realized that today might be her last day on earth. Her life was in Roman's hands right now. She thought about Shane. Was he even in this warehouse or had that only been a ruse? By who? She thought about Jason and felt her heart break. Would she ever see him again? They'd left on a terrible note. Would that be the thing he would remember after she was gone?

Stop it, Phoebe. You're not dead yet.

"Roman, is your father here? I would like to talk to him. I'm sure he could clear this all up." *What am I saying? Niklaus Mitrofanov is a mobster kingpin, a killer.* But she needed time. Her attorney skills kicked into gear. That was all she had that might save them. She needed to get to the top, to the man who could make decisions. That meant she needed to see Niklaus.

Roman's eyes narrowed for a moment. Had she overstepped? Then he smiled. "I think father would like to see you, too. You and Sheriff Wolfe's brothers." He stepped up to the keypad and entered in some numbers.

As the door swung open, Mitrofanov's men pushed her, Mitchell, and Lucas forward.

In the center of the windowless room was Shane, sitting in a metal folding chair with his hands tied behind his back. Both his eyes were black and his lips were swollen. Niklaus stood beside him with a gun pointed to Shane's head.

She twisted free of the man holding her and ran forward. The thug who had come through the door with Roman earlier caught her before she could get to her brother. *Oh God. Please.*

"You let a woman best you, Oleg." Roman taunted the man she'd escaped. "Thankfully, Peter was here to help."

Oleg glared at him but slinked back to the side of the metal door.

"Hand our guest over to me, Peter," the balding, fat mobster said.

The thug passed her to Niklaus, who grabbed her by the arm. Peter then stepped back beside Roman.

Niklaus smiled. "Ms. Blue, I'm shocked to see you."

Shane choked out, "Sis, you shouldn't be here."

"I came because of your text, Shane."

"What text?"

The men holding Lucas and Mitchell pulled them behind her and to the side.

"Did you get your hands on a cell phone without my knowledge, Mr. Blue?" Niklaus slammed the butt of his gun into his face.

"Stop it," she screamed, horrified by what she was witnessing.

"Father, Blue has never been left alone." Roman moved on the other side of Shane, opposite Niklaus. "There is no way he could send a text to anyone."

"That better be true, Roman." Niklaus's face darkened. "We need to wrap up our business here quickly and get back to your brother." He placed the barrel of his gun at Shane's temple.

"Don't hurt him," she pleaded, tears rolling down her face. "Please. Tell me what I can do to stop this."

"Maybe you can help, Ms. Blue. I haven't been able to get your brother to talk. With you here, I think he might…how do you say it in English…sing like a pigeon? Your brother has been working with an enemy of mine. You've heard of him, I'm sure. Mr. Kip Lunceford. Pity. Kip and I were friends once. But like everyone else, he wanted my diamonds."

"I can't believe this. Shane, tell me this isn't true." *You can't be mixed up with Lunceford, too. You just can't.*

Shane turned to her but didn't say a word. She noticed he was twisting his wrists in the ropes. He was trying to get free.

The mobster laughed. "Roman, who are these other men?"

"Sheriff Wolfe's brothers," his son answered.

"Isn't this my lucky day. I knew the sheriff would come looking for my diamonds, but I had no idea he would recruit his brothers to help." Mitrofanov glared at Lucas and Mitchell. "The jewels aren't here, boys. They are safe and being guarded by my other son, Anton. Too bad for you. Where is your brother, gentlemen?"

The metal door swung open, revealing Jason and Corey with their guns drawn.

Her first thought was how happy she was to see both of them, but the one that followed, the rational one, made her heart stop.

Outgunned and outnumbered.

Nothing had changed. Their chances of surviving Mitrofanov and his men were trifling.

"Sheriff Wolfe, I see you are joining the party," Niklaus said. "As you can see, there are six of us and only two of you. Use your head and put down your weapons."

"Not on your life, Mitrofanov," he said, his gun aimed directly at the mobster's head.

Her heart thudded in her chest. Something was going to tip the scales and end this standoff. She couldn't see how things would land in their favor.

"Niklaus Mitrofanov, I am a US marshal," Corey said. "Don't make this any worse than it already is."

"Ah. You must be this scumbag's brother, too. All the Blue siblings under one roof. My roof." Niklaus's tone told her he was losing patience. "I'll say this one more time, gentlemen. Put down your weapons."

The steel in their eyes gave their answer.

"Please, Corey, put your gun down. Jason, I love you. Do as he says. I beg you."

"I can't do that, baby." Jason's tone was gentle but firm.

"Lovers? You and Ms. Blue? Sheriff, I had no idea." Niklaus grabbed her, pulling her against his fat body, placing the barrel of his gun to her head.

She held her breath, believing this was her last moment on earth. Time seemed to slow to a crawl.

Shocked, she heard the back door open and all of them glanced that direction.

Joshua Phong and another man ran in.

Out of the corner of her eye, she saw Mitchell and Lucas use the opportunity the diversion had given them, elbowing the men holding them in their guts, sending the bastards to the ground.

In the very next instant, her men were pulling her free from Niklaus, who was aiming his gun directly at her. They covered her with their bodies as Jason fired at the bastard.

As shots rang out everywhere around her, she saw the mobster's eyes widen, his gun tumbling to the ground. Mitrofanov slumped over, dead.

She screamed when she saw Roman point his gun at Jason.

Shane, now free of his restraints, jumped in front of Niklaus's son, taking the bullet meant for Jason.

"No. God, no. Let me go." She struggled to run to Shane, but Lucas held her tight. "Please. I have to get to my brother."

Roman, the last of Mitrofanov's men still standing, swung his gun her direction.

Before the bastard could get a shot off, Jason killed him.

* * * *

Jason ran to Phoebe, who was already leaning over her brother, his friend.

She pulled out her cell and punched in 911. "Talk to me, Shane."

"Black will come, sis," Shane whispered, and then closed his eyes. Thank God he was still breathing.

"What did he mean by that, Jason?"

"No clue." Jason ripped off his shirt, twisting it into a ball and placing it on the wound in Shane's chest.

"My fucking phone is dead." Her face was filled with alarm.

"Use mine, sweetheart. It's in my left pocket."

The room was littered with four bodies—Niklaus, his son, and two of his henchmen. The other two, who had been holding Mitchell and Lucas, had surrendered. Corey placed them in handcuffs. Josh was helping Agent Smith, who had also taken a bullet in the shoulder.

Phoebe touched his arm. "Jason, your phone is dead, too."

"Fuck." He wasn't about to let Shane die. His old friend had just saved his life.

Keeping his shirt, which was now soaked in blood, pressed to Shane's chest with one hand, he reached into his pocket and pulled out his ROC. He'd already run through the security prompts before coming inside the warehouse to be ready to get in touch with Brown at a moment's notice. "Use this, baby."

She took it and began to dial.

Lucas and Mitchell came up beside him, stripping off their shirts to place on top of his.

Don't die on me, Shane.

"This isn't working either." The panic in Phoebe's voice was obvious to him.

Before he could try to calm her down, the two metal doors closed, their locks engaging.

"Oh my God." Phoebe stared at Brown's device. She swung it around to him so he could see.

Kip Lunceford's smiling face filled the screen.

"He's on mine, too, Jason," Corey said.

"Here, too," Agent Smith informed.

"Hello, Sheriff." Kip's twisted smile filled Jason with disgust.

"Is this live?" Josh asked.

"Young Mr. Phong, I can assure you this is very live," Kip taunted.

Jason looked up to the ceiling and saw the cameras. "That's how he's seeing us."

Was the fucker in St. Louis? Were Brown and the rest of the team closing in without his knowledge?

"You are correct, Sherriff, about the cameras. That and your CIA top-of-the-line devices."

"How did you hack into them, Lunceford?" Agent Smith asked.

"Like taking candy from a baby, Neil. Now, if you will all just be quiet for a moment, I will tell you why you are here."

Jason felt rage roll up inside him like a tsunami. "You want us to believe you had something to do with this, Kip? Bullshit."

"You underestimate me, Sheriff. I had everything to do with it."

"You're lying, asshole" Corey cursed. "You might've been watching from the cameras when we came in here, but Jason and I came to Chicago to find my brother."

"True, Marshal. You came because of the photograph I sent the lovely Joanne Brown, didn't you? Little did you know, Shane had a gun to his back." The motherfucker smiled. "Photoshop has helped me more than you can know."

"Son of a bitch," Corey shot back.

Kip frowned. "My mother is dead, Marshal. That's not nice to say about her."

Lunceford had killed his parents. He didn't give a fuck about anyone.

"Get on with what you have to say, Lunceford, and be done with it." Jason noticed Phoebe's hand was shaking, but she continued holding the ROC so he could see it.

"Please, Mr. Lunceford, unlock the doors," she pleaded. "My brother needs an ambulance."

"Ms. Blue, it's so nice to see you, but you are wrong about your brother. All of you have been so wrong."

Jason wondered what the creep meant by that.

"He's been shot," Phoebe choked out. "Can't you see that from the cameras? He *does* need medical attention."

"Unfortunately, he won't survive today, Ms. Blue." Lunceford cleared his throat as if he was about to deliver a sermon. "I'll get back to your brother and what I know about him, but first, let me begin with how I came up with this brilliant plan. It all began with Niklaus trying to stiff me of my money."

"It wasn't your money," Jason said. "It was TBK's."

Lunceford shook his head. "You're wrong again. I am the reason TBK exists. I was there in the early years. They are still using my platforms for many of their programs. I wanted my just rewards. Using some contacts I had, I was able to get a meeting with Mitrofanov."

How far is Lunceford's reach? Jason bristled but held his tongue.

"Pulling the Russian's strings was child's play. I played on Niklaus's ego and greed. We both had one thing in common. We want to burn Destiny and all its citizens to the ground."

"Stop wasting our time, Lunceford." Jason despised the bastard. Somehow they'd fallen into Kip's trap, but it was his duty to make sure they all came out alive. "We know that already."

"Fuck off, Kip." Josh stood. "I'm going to get us out of here." He went to the keypad and Corey joined him.

Mitchell and Lucas headed to the other one by the front door.

"Knock yourself out, Mr. Phong. The only way to open the doors now is from the other side. You killed Mitrofanov's men. No one is coming."

"You bastard," Phoebe shouted.

"Where was I?" Kip asked, ignoring her. "Ah, yes. When Niklaus made it clear that he was going to keep the five million for himself, I engaged my plan. I always have several contingencies in place. It's a game to me, folks. And I always win. Like now. Ms. Blue, did you know that I'm the one behind the Braxton suit against Steele Ranch? Of course you didn't. An associate of mine, God rest his heroin-addicted soul, took on the identity I set up for him."

"Mr. Harrison Rutledge. You knew him?"

"No. I created him. A fictional character that I knew Braxton would hire. I'm very proud of my creation. Rutledge is one of my best works."

"Why? What do you have against Jennifer Steele?" Phoebe asked.

"Only that she is a citizen of Destiny, but that wasn't the reason I got the ball rolling with the lawsuit. It was part of my contingency plan, Ms. Blue. Braxton's headquarters are in Chicago. Niklaus's base of operation was also in Chicago. Are you catching on? It was my plan all along to get you here when I deemed necessary. That's why my associate requested the deposition to be this morning. Then I sent you a text from your dear brother, and, *voila*, you came. My plan worked perfectly."

Knowing Lunceford had been pulling strings to get to Phoebe enraged Jason. "I will kill you, asshole. I will find you. You won't be able to hide. I will rip you to shreds."

"Which brings me to another part of my plan, which also turned out just the way I wanted. Sheriff, I'm so glad to see that you and your brothers are back with Ms. Blue. Anyone can see you belong together."

"You had nothing to do with that, motherfucker." Mitchell's emotions were clearly raw and full of rage.

"But on the contrary, I had everything to do with it. Mr. McCrae and I became friends quite a while ago."

"No fucking way." Lucas's eyes were filled with rage.

"Yes, fucking way. I wanted to be able to get the sheriff to Chicago, too. With you and Mitchell. Life is like a chess game, gentlemen. I'm hundreds of moves ahead of my opponents—that's everyone from Destiny—at all times. Poor McCrae. He was in love with you, Phoebe. Truly. A deluded fool, but harmless. Andy believed I would be able to get you to fall in love with him, Ms. Blue. I'm sure I could have, but that didn't fit into my plan. When McCrae went off script and sent those roses, he almost ruined all of my work. I had to bring in another associate to retire him."

How many people does Lunceford have working for him?

"Sheriff, you surprised me when you pocketed Mr. Blue's wallet. So unlike you. Fake identifications are so easy to get these days." Lunceford laughed.

Jason's pulse pounded hot. He'd been played by the fucker.

"Having my associate plant that billfold worked exactly as I thought it would. You thought Shane was the murderer. The photo of him and Mitrofanov got you to Chicago exactly when I wanted." Kip's face darkened. "Which brings me to Shane Blue. All of you judged him. Three years in prison for a crime he didn't commit."

Kip's words shocked and sliced him in two.

Phoebe's eyes were wide. "What? You did that to my brother? He's innocent of everything?"

"Actually, he isn't, at least not to me. Shane and a Mr. Black teamed up, unbeknownst to any of you. The drug dealing charge was a ruse. The CIA wanted someone on the inside of the prison to get close to me. Fools. Shane was one of the best undercover agents I've ever run across, but I'm better. In fact, I'm the best."

Shane was an undercover agent. Everything that had happened had been orchestrated by Mr. Black. Jason looked down at his friend, seeing him in a new light. Even what had gone down in the diner must've been to push him away. Shane had a mission to do. *Three years in prison? My God, you're a fucking hero. No wonder nothing made sense about what happened back then.*

"Shane muddled many of my plans. Finally, I had a competitor that was worthy of my merit. But of course, I figured out who he really was. That's why I made sure he made his parole. I'm certain Black, God rest his soul, and Shane were surprised by that outcome."

"Jason," Phoebe whispered in a panicky tone. "Shane's breathing is shallow."

He noticed it, too. The guys weren't having any luck getting the door open. "Get on with it, Lunceford."

"Anxious? Sheriff, you're one man who is normally calm under pressure." The bastard's lips twisted into an evil grin. "The finale of my genius orchestration was this. I wanted the diamonds. I wanted to pay Shane back for what he'd done to me. I wanted to pay all of you back. After my escape, I needed you here to distract Niklaus. He was so paranoid, continually moving the diamonds from one location to another. Timing was critical. Making him think I was working with Shane to get the diamonds was my first move. Niklaus took the bait and sent his men to grab Shane. Besides these cameras, I have an insider in Mitrofanov's organization that is my eyes and ears."

"Niklaus's other son." Jason was putting all the pieces together in Lunceford's horrific puzzle. "Anton Mitrofanov."

"Excellent, Sheriff. You and Shane might be the best opponents I've ever faced. My second move was getting you to the house that Brown incorrectly thought was Mitrofanov's headquarters. It was actually owned by another associate of mine. She left the laptop with the photo of Shane with the gun to his head. Accidentally…on purpose." The psycho laughed. "Once I had all of you in place, all I had to do was pull the trigger. I sent a message to Niklaus. I was coming to get my friend Shane. I knew he would take him to his main base of operation, the warehouse you are in, and leave the diamonds with Anton. But I needed him to be distracted long enough for me to get the jewels and get away. That's where all of you came in." The maniac laughed again and held up his hand, which held a fistful of diamonds. "Check mate."

They all heard a hissing sound.

"Now, open the damn doors, Lunceford."

"I'm free. No more prisons for me. Now, I will burn down your town, but I'll take my time. That's all part of the joy of the game." Kip smiled. "I will miss you, Sheriff. I will especially miss Shane. Good-bye, Destonians. It's been fun."

The screen went blank and Jason smelled the toxic fumes billowing into the room.

Chapter Sixteen

Jason put his arm around Phoebe. "Get low to the floor, baby."

"What difference will that make? Lunceford won. It's over." She held Shane's hand.

"We are not giving up. You're strong, sweetheart." He kept his tone steady, knowing she needed reassurance. "We will get through this." *We must.*

"Yes, Sir. I hope you're right. But just in case, I need to tell you something."

He placed his finger on her lips. "I'm the one who needs to tell you something first. I'm sorry, baby. I love you so much. You were always right. I was so wrong. About everything." The effect of the gas was making him lightheaded.

"I love you, too. I'm sorry. I was just as wrong." She coughed several times. "Jason, it's getting hard for me to breathe."

"We need to get down right now." He helped her to the floor and held her close.

"It's hopeless, Jason. Lunceford has won. I know that now. We're all going to die. I want Mitchell and Lucas with us. Please."

He looked at his brothers, who were working frantically on one of the keypads. The pride and love he felt for Lucas and Mitchell had never faltered. "They are trying to save us, baby. They won't give up. You and I both know that."

"I know. Looks like Corey and Josh are trying, too." Tears rolled from Phoebe's eyes as she placed her hand over Shane's unmoving lips to check on his breathing. "He's still with us, Jason. Please God, let the doors open."

"He's strong, baby. Just like his sister." *I'm sorry, buddy.* Shane had been a hero all along and Jason had never known it. But there was no time left to tell Shane how proud he was of him. There would be no more fishing trips. He would never have a chance to ask Shane to be his best man when he, Lucas, and Mitchell married his sister.

"I'm trying to have faith, Jason, but it's so hard."

He kissed her, knowing that they'd only just found each other again. But their lives were about to end. There would be no future, no family. These last few moments were the only ones he had left with the woman of his dreams. He didn't want her to be scared. He was her Dom. It was his job to make her feel safe. *I thank God she knows how much I love her.* "It might take a miracle, baby, but I know you believe in them."

"You came back to me. We're together again. I do believe in miracles, Jason."

They all heard banging from the other side of both doors.

"Make some noise," he ordered. "We need to let whoever is out there know we are in here."

All of them yelled.

Suddenly, both doors burst open, letting in fresh air, a medical team, CIA agents, and a person who he never expected to see again—Agent Black.

Am I hallucinating? I must've taken in more gas than I thought.

"Over here," he called to a couple of the EMTs. They took over, caring for Shane.

"Take these two to the van," Black commanded, pointing to the two Mitrofanov men still alive. "The rest are friendlies. Get them outside. We need to secure this location and find the source of the gas and shut it down."

He and Phoebe followed the stretcher the EMTs had put Shane on.

Mitchell and Lucas came up beside him and Phoebe.

"You okay, baby?" Mitchell asked.

She nodded.

He and his brothers grabbed her, holding her between them.

She's safe.

Agent Black walked up to them. "Sheriff."

"Black, what the hell? You're not dead?"

"Let me get this taken care of and I will fill you in on the details, Jason. I need to notify Jo Brown that all of you are okay."

"Has she known you were alive all this time?"

"No, but I was keeping tabs on all she was doing."

One of the agents ran up to Black. "Sir, command is on the horn and wants to talk to you."

"I've got to go, but I will meet you at the hospital as soon as possible."

Jason held out his hand. "I'm glad you're alive, Easton."

Black shook his hand. "Jason, the feeling is mutual."

* * * *

Phoebe felt like she'd been holding her breath since seeing the text from Shane. The waiting was killing her. Shane was still in surgery. Agent Smith's surgery was over. He was doing fine.

Please God, let Shane be fine, too.

She sat between Jason and Lucas in the waiting room. Mitchell sat directly across from her talking to Ashley on his cell. Corey and Josh had just left to find all of them something to eat. Though it had been many hours since her last meal, she couldn't imagine eating anything with her stomach tied up in knots.

Her parents were headed this way, but wouldn't be here for at least a couple more hours. Hopefully, Shane would be out of surgery by then. She and Corey had called their parents with the news about Shane, but there wasn't much to tell about his condition.

"That's right, Ashley," Mitchell said into his phone.

Her guys were taking charge, clearly realizing that she'd dealt with all she could tonight.

Mitchell ended the call. "Ashley will be here shortly, honey."

She turned to Jason. "I've been such a fool. Will you ever forgive me?"

"Forgive you? I'm the one who needs to be forgiven. Look what I've done to you."

"None of us knew what Shane was doing, but I was stubborn. He kept writing and calling me, telling me to go on with my life with you, Mitchell, and Lucas. But I just couldn't. I blamed all three of you, but you most of all, Jason. Why wouldn't you ever tell me what happened between you and Shane at the diner?"

"Baby, I thought I was protecting you. I was shocked at Shane's behavior. I went to the diner to try to talk some sense into him. I wanted to take him right then to rehab. He laughed at me, saying he loved drugs and the money that came with them. He told me he would never stop no matter what." Jason sighed. "Now I know it was only an act. When I said to him that he was going to ruin you, Corey, and your parents' lives, he hauled off and hit me. That's when I thought he was completely lost. I made up my mind that I needed to do whatever I could to get him away from you. I knew it would hurt you, but I believed it was the only choice I had." Jason closed his eyes. "I was scared Shane would eventually overdose."

She squeezed his hand. "I know you care about him as much as I do."

"I love you, Phoebe," Jason said, opening his eyes. "I've always loved you."

She kissed him, tears rolling down her cheeks. "I never stopped loving you, Jason."

"I love you, bro," Mitchell said. "We all made mistakes."

"That's the truth," Lucas added. "Jason, you know I love you, brother."

"I love you, guys." Jason smiled. "No one would guess we were big bad Doms, would they?"

They all laughed.

She leaned into Jason. "After coming so close to death, I think it's okay if we go overboard a little with the 'I love yous,' don't you agree?"

"I do, sweetheart."

"The truth is, guys, I can't hear you say it enough," she confessed.

Lucas touched her cheek. "I love you, baby."

She kissed his fingers. "I love you, too."

Mitchell leaned forward and grabbed her hands. "God, I love you so much."

She smiled. "I love you so much, too."

Having her three men back in her life meant everything to her. But she still felt like her world was crumbling. Shane was in surgery. *Please, God. Let him live.*

She sat quietly for several minutes, her insides a complete jumble.

Agent Black walked into the waiting room. "Sorry it took so long for me to get here. How's Shane doing?"

"Still in surgery," Jason told him. "Have a seat."

"Yes, Mr. Black. I have a ton of questions for you," she told him.

"I'm sure you all do," he said, sitting beside Mitchell.

"Maybe you should start with how you are still alive," Jason said. "How did you get out of Mitrofanov's house before it blew up?"

"Shane is how, Jason. He and I have been working together for a long time. I told him what was going down and he remained hidden but within striking distance. He and Dylan Strange are the best agents I've ever seen."

"I still can't believe Shane was working for the CIA the whole time he was in prison." How had he kept that secret for so long from her and the rest of the family?

"He was, Phoebe. I met him through Dylan about five years ago. Dylan was getting out of the Agency and your brother wanted to get in."

"I never knew that."

Jason put his arm around her. "I didn't know about the CIA, but since we were kids, Shane had always told me he wanted to be in law enforcement. We both did." Jason turned to Agent Black. "Everything is starting to make sense. Go on."

"Shane came on board and started training."

Phoebe remembered the time Shane left Destiny for about six months. "That was when he said he was working for a technology company back east."

"His cover, yes. A year later, I got intel that Lunceford was working with terrorist organizations even though he was incarcerated in the federal prison system. The bastard had proven again and again that he could get out any time he liked. Several murders later, including his own parents, I put a plan together to try to stop him. Since Shane was from Destiny, the home of TBK's headquarters, the last place Kip had been employed, I went to him with my plan. Being a friend to the Knights, whose company had suffered so much because of Lunceford, Shane jumped at the idea and volunteered."

Jason sighed. "So you sent him to prison to keep tabs on Kip. Did Dylan ever know about this?"

"No. He wasn't with the Agency back then."

"But he is now," Jason said.

"He is?" she asked.

"You just blew Strange's cover, Sheriff," Black said with a laugh. "No worries. I think your girl can be trusted."

"She can, but I'm not so sure about my brothers," he teased.

"I know how to keep a secret," Mitchell shot back, smiling.

"And of course I do," Lucas added.

"That's very good to know." Black rubbed his chin. Was he thinking about recruiting them? "When Dylan sought me out after Kip's ex, Megan, came to Destiny to try to locate the prison Kip was in, I gave Dylan the file but redacted Shane's name from it. The CIA has a strict need-to-know practice, and I didn't believe Dylan met the requirement at that time."

"Why three years?" Phoebe felt the weight of all the time she'd lost with Shane and with the Wolfe brothers in the center of her chest.

"That was what Shane wanted. He was only supposed to stay undercover for six months. Your brother stopped a terrorist plot that would've taken out ten thousand or more innocent lives. Kip was involved, though we never were able to prove it."

"He's a slippery bastard," Jason said.

"That he is, Sheriff. I was ready to extract Shane from the prison, but he had gotten wind of more things Kip was doing. Shane convinced me to leave him in. You have no idea how many lives have been saved because of Shane Blue."

"He's a fucking hero," Jason said in a tone of awe.

"Yes, he is." Black nodded. "Back then, Lunceford's network was even more extensive than it is now."

"With five million in diamonds, he's going to be able to rebuild fast," Mitchell said.

"Yes. And with Mitrofanov's only living son on his team, it's going to be hard to bring him down. Shane and I were trying to get to the diamonds, believing it would lead to Lunceford. Our plan didn't work."

Lucas leaned forward. "Shane wanted to be captured by Mitrofanov?"

"That's right. He had one of the best tracking devices the Agency has in the heel of his boot. When I couldn't locate him, I activated it. That's how I found him and you."

Carrying food, Corey and Josh walked into the room.

The doctor came in right behind them. "Everything went perfectly. Shane is going to be fine."

Chapter Seventeen

Phoebe saw Shane's eyes open for the first time since the warehouse disaster. "Mom, wake up. Shane's coming to."

Her mom and her dads had arrived in Chicago late the night before. They'd all stayed by Shane's beside, too worried to leave him alone.

Phoebe watched as her mom jumped from the recliner next to her and moved to Shane's hospital bed. Her dads and Corey stood on the opposite side.

"You're going to be okay, sweetheart," her mom said. "Shane, the doctors say you are just fine."

"Mom?" He blinked several times, clearly trying to focus his vision.

"I'm here."

Dad Curtis touched him lightly on the shoulder. "Son, your brother and sister are here, too, and so are Dad Eddie and me."

"What happened?" he asked.

Phoebe leaned in. "You were shot trying to protect Jason, Shane. Do you remember the warehouse and Mitrofanov and his men?"

"Yes, it's coming to me now."

"You're a hero, baby." Her mom kissed him on the cheek. "A CIA agent. I'm so proud of you. I always knew there was something fishy about your story. You never could lie to your mother."

"You were the hardest one to convince, mom. And I guess I really didn't succeed."

"No, honey. You didn't."

"So my cover has been blown. How did you find out?"

"Black," Corey told him. "You're a fucking hero."

"Corey Lee Blue, watch your mouth," her mom scolded.

"Sorry, mom, but it's true."

She grinned. "Yes, it is."

"Son, we are all so proud of you." Dad smiled broadly. "You can't imagine how happy we were to learn everything you've done."

"I'm sorry for all I put you through. I just had to."

"Yes, you did, Shane." Phoebe was so honored to be his sister. "You saved so many lives."

"Thanks, Phoebe. You suffered most of all though. I hated to see what happened between you and the Wolfes." His eyebrows shot up. "They were at the warehouse, too, weren't they? I remember."

"Yes," she told him.

"Where are they now? I want to see them."

Corey nodded. "They're right outside this door."

Her mom leaned down and kissed Shane on the cheek. "I'll let them come in and we will be right outside, son. Phoebe, you stay here."

Her parents and Corey walked out. A moment later, her three wonderful men walked in.

* * * *

Jason walked straight to Shane's bed. "I'm so sorry, bro. I should've trusted you. I should've believed in you."

"So does that mean I should've won an Academy Award for best actor?" Shane smiled. "I also am sorry for what I put you through, Jason. You're my best friend. But that terrorist plot had to be stopped. It was bigger than any of us."

"I heard. My God, you're a fucking hero."

"So, I've been told recently." He laughed. "I'm so sorry, guys. I never dreamed that my mission would break you and my sister up."

Jason put his arm around Phoebe. "Water under the bridge,

buddy."

"I'm so glad you are back together again. You belong with each other."

"Yes, we do," Lucas agreed.

"Damn right, we do," Mitchell added. "We're waiting for you to get back on your feet to be our best man at our wedding."

"I'd like to be asked first, if you don't mind," Phoebe teased. "But my answer is a resounding *yes.*"

"To be best man? We would rather Shane take that role," Mitchell shot back. "I thought you would rather be the bride, baby."

"You devil. You know what I mean."

"Fill me in, fellows," Shane said. "Did we get Mitrofanov? And what about the diamonds? Is Lunceford in custody?"

"Slow down, Shane," Jason said, happy to see his old friend so lively. "We don't want to tire you."

"So you'd rather I just lie here and wonder? Come on."

"He's got a point, Jason," Mitchell said.

They told him everything that had happened at the warehouse after he'd been shot.

"Damn it, that bastard is still out there." Shane looked at Jason. "I know you had been working hard to bring Mitrofanov down for some time. I'm glad you got your man."

"I'm glad you saved my life, bro."

"I would do it again in a fucking minute. I will always have your back. You know, Jason, since Kip has declared war on Destiny, we all have to work together."

"I plan on deputizing every single citizen. We're going to get the motherfucker."

The door opened and the doctor came in. "Only two visitors at a time, please. My patient needs his rest."

Chapter Eighteen

"I am so proud of Lucas." Phoebe loved seeing the whole town come out to pay tribute to one of her men.

She sat with some of her favorite friends in folding chairs. All the guys in town, including Jason and Mitchell, were setting up the area for the groundbreaking ceremony.

"You should be," Amber said. "He's the big man around town these days, that's for sure."

"You have to come up and see what he's done for the Boys Ranch." Belle's eyes widened. "It's amazing."

Phoebe knew she was more than a little interested in two Destonian men. "That's what my brothers told me after you gave them the tour of the place."

Belle smiled. "I've given lots of tours."

She liked Belle very much but wondered if a woman who had grown up outside of Destiny would understand the kind of life her brothers would want. "Are you still planning to open the Boys Ranch by Christmas?"

"Absolutely. We have several more boys arriving by then." Belle was a woman who had the heart of a mother, though she had no children of her own. The way she took care of Juan and the other orphan boys was something to behold.

"Ladies and gentlemen, the groundbreaking ceremony for our new hospital will commence in five minutes," Patrick O'Leary announced from the temporary stage that had been set up for the event.

"Looks like the entire town has turned out for the festivities," Megan said.

"Don't you mean the entire county, Megan?" Nicole asked. "Why not? Lucas has designed an amazing building to replace the old clinic."

"Did you see the model he made of how it's going to look? It's going to be a showstopper. I wouldn't be surprised if your man doesn't win some architectural award, Phoebe."

"That would be something." She'd grown so close to Amber, Megan, and Nicole, all of whom had come to Destiny from other places. They'd found love in the arms of men she'd grown up with all her life. *Why couldn't Belle do the same?* Shane and Corey certainly were interested in her.

Erica grinned. "When will we be seeing you walk down the aisle, Miss Blue? Isn't it about time you made honest men out of the Wolfe brothers?"

"You only care because you want to be my maid of honor, right?"

"I'd settle for bridesmaid," she said with a laugh.

Like her, Erica had lived in Destiny her whole life, but her past had been much more difficult. She'd lost her parents in the plane crash that took out some of the best citizens that the town still mourned to this day.

"The Wolfe brothers were sort of talking about a wedding," Ashley told them. "At the hospital in Chicago."

"Ash, can't you keep a secret? I swear to God, I should dock your pay," Phoebe teased.

"You would be lost without me, boss, and you know it."

"True."

"How is Shane doing?" Belle looked honestly concerned.

Maybe she would be perfect for my brothers. "He's doing great. The doctors are amazed at how fast he's recovering. It's only been two weeks, but he's zooming through the physical therapy sessions."

"That's good to hear, Phoebe."

Mitchell's band took the stage.

"Betty's daughter looks stunning," Gretchen said. "Look at all the single men gawking at her."

"Too bad for them," Ethel chimed in. "Kaylyn only cares about her work."

"She trains guide dogs, doesn't she?" Jena was the newest member to their girl pack.

"That's right, and does an amazing job of it, too," Erica said. "See those two guys over there with the German shepherds? Those are hers."

Gretchen smiled wickedly. "The dogs or the men?"

They all laughed.

"The black guy is Chance," Ethel said. "Betty told me that Kaylyn has been mooning over him for years. Chance was born blind. He educates adults who lose their sight later in life."

"The other man is my old partner, Jaris." Nicole's guilty feelings could be seen on her face. "He's a wonderful man. I hate what happened to him."

"Honey, we all do," Megan said. "But look at him with his dog. He's going to be fine."

Jaris's bravery was unquestioned. The whole town knew what he'd done that day when the crazy woman had tried to shoot Nicole. Phoebe wasn't sure if he would decide to settle here, but she knew every person in town was trying to convince him to stay.

Gretchen lowered her voice. "Word on the street is that Kaylyn likes Jaris, too."

Ethel shook her head and grinned. "Where did you hear that, Gretchen Hollingsworth?"

"I have my sources, Your Honor."

The men started filing into the rows of chairs, taking their seats next to their wives and girlfriends.

Emmett, Cody, and Bryant Stone sat with Amber, who was expecting. Their child was due June of next year. Scott and Eric placed Megan in between them. The two billionaire brothers never looked happier. Nicole sat between her men, Sawyer and Reed. Those cowboys had found their perfect match in Destiny's newest deputy. Cameron sat with Erica, but Dylan, wearing his ever-present sunglasses, remained standing. Those two men were alike in many ways and not so much in other ways, but it was clear to Phoebe and the whole town, they belonged with Erica. Jena's guys, Matt and Sean, walked to her with her mom and little Kimmie. Those five were Destiny's newest residents, and everyone welcomed them with open arms.

"Hey, sweetheart." Jason sat down next to her.

"Hi, honey."

He put his arm around her shoulders. "Big turnout for Lucas, isn't it?"

"Very big. I'm so proud of him."

"This might be the biggest audience Mitchell's band has ever played for," Jason said. "Look, baby. Here comes both my brothers."

She watched Mitchell and Lucas leave the stage and head straight for her. God, this was her dream. She'd walked away from them three years ago like a fool, but thank God the love her men had for her was stronger than she'd ever imagined. Her heart belonged to them completely.

"Honey, the band is going to play a new song," Mitchell told her. "It's one I wrote for you, and it is *our* sound."

"Shouldn't you have written one for me?" Lucas winked at her. "This is my day, baby. Right?"

"Yes, it is," Mitchell said. "We are all proud of you, bro."

Jason smiled. "You've definitely lifted up the Wolfe name around town, Lucas."

"That coming from a man who has an election coming next year," Lucas teased. "Glad to help."

Mitchell waved to the band and they started playing.

She could tell something was not on the up and up. "Mitchell, shouldn't you be up there with the rest of Wolfe Mayhem?"

He grabbed her hand. "Actually, we're all going to the stage."

She looked at her three men, their loving eyes on her. "What's this all about?"

Jason stood. "You're about to find out, sweetheart."

As they headed to the front, Kaylyn started singing the song Mitchell had written for Phoebe.

Phoebe's heart swelled hearing the romantic words.

As we begin our life together,
The love we share,
Witnessed by the stars above,
Grows stronger with each and every kiss.
We will give you all our tomorrows,
Forever, until time no longer exists.

Standing in front of the whole town, Phoebe's eyes were filled with happy tears seeing Jason, Lucas, and Mitchell get on their knees.

"Phoebe Lynn Blue, will you do us the honor of becoming our wife?" they asked in unison.

"Yes, Jason. Yes, Lucas. Yes, Mitchell. I want to marry you. With all my heart."

The crowd roared their approval as her men hugged her tight.

The loneliness of the past three years was no more. She glanced at her parents and saw her mom dotting her eyes.

This is where I belong.

Chapter Nineteen

Phoebe grinned, seeing her men running around like roosters in her living room. Their chests had remained puffed up since she'd accepted their proposal earlier that day. Her every need was met by them. If she even hinted that she wanted anything, they had it in her hand. She was surprised they let her brush her own teeth.

When they brought her another piece of cake and cup of coffee, she had to say something. "What's up with you three today?"

Mitchell held up his hands, clearly faking surprise at her question. "What do you mean by that, baby?"

She pointed to the cake and coffee. "Case in point, gentlemen."

"We love to spoil you, honey," Lucas said.

Jason put his arm around her. "What's wrong with that?"

"Nothing. But since this morning, you've been going overboard. Please. Tell me. What's up?"

Mitchell smiled. "We have a surprise for you, sweetheart."

Jason kissed her. "We're taking you to Phase Four for a special evening."

"You are?" Eagerness swelled inside her. "Is that why you've kept me moving from one of your beds to the other instead of sharing me like I've been asking?"

They all three grinned. "Yes, baby," they said in unison.

* * * *

Jason watched Phoebe's chest rise and fall as her breathing increased and the corners of her lips curled up slightly. When she licked them, he knew he'd been right in setting up the scene on the main stage for her. She was clearly vibrating with excitement at the idea of being put on display.

Phase Four had a few members milling around, but it wouldn't be long before the crowd would arrive.

Mitchell grinned, placing his hands on her breasts. "I can just imagine what is going on in that pretty little head."

Lucas stood behind her. "You don't have to be a mind reader to know that." He lifted her leather mini, which the three of them had chosen for her. Since she wore no panties, his brother's fingers had free access to her flesh. "She's already wet."

Jason cupped her chin, enjoying the flood of red that came to her cheeks. "We have big plans for you, baby. We're going to tie you up, spank your ass, shock your nipples, clamp your clit, use plugs, paddles and whips on your soft, silky body."

He could see her pulse fluttering in the sides of her neck at the list of lusty exploits they were going to give her.

"How are you doing, sweetheart?" Mitchell asked her quietly, though just loud enough for Jason to hear.

He held in his smile.

"I'm good, Sir." Phoebe needed Mitchell's sensitivity as much as she needed his and Lucas's dominance.

Mitchell enjoyed the life, but his dominant side had a softer edge than most. Lucas fell somewhere between him and Mitchell. He loved the lifestyle, but didn't feel the need to dominate as strongly as Jason did. Phoebe responded to that as well. He smiled, knowing she also responded beautifully to his type of dominance, ever demanding and never letting up.

"Center stage, sub," he commanded, holding onto the chain that was hooked to her collar.

"Yes, Master." Phoebe stared at him as if he was the last drop of water and she was dying of thirst.

He was both thirsty and starving for her. God knew she was the tastiest morsel he'd ever dined on, and by the looks on his two brothers faces, it was clear they felt the same way. After three years of famine, they were finally back together. Sharing her with his brothers had always been the dream. She'd always been in his heart. She was the right woman for him, the only woman. He loved her and would never let her go again.

Lucas gave him a slight nod. He and Mitchell pulled the bench to the center, getting the floor set up for the scene they'd planned for her.

He pulled her in tight to his frame, enjoying the feel of her nipples against his bare skin, causing his cock to harden in his leather pants. Unlike his brothers, who both wore black vests, he was bare chested. "Time to get you tied up, baby."

Phoebe smiled and nodded. When she saw the paddles and crops that Lucas and Mitchell were pulling out of their satchels, she began nibbling on her lower lip.

Knowing she needed a moment, he offered her his hand. "It's been a long time since you've been on this stage, hasn't it?" He remembered the first time he'd brought her here. They both were fairly new to BDSM. Though inexperienced, that was the very night they realized the lifestyle was for them.

"Yes, Sir." The tremor of excitement and anxiety he detected in her voice told him she needed a moment before they strapped her to the bench. "A very long time."

He squeezed her hand, and she released a lungful of air. She'd been holding her breath. "Baby, I know this is a big moment."

She nodded, and her face softened. "Very big, Master. I've only been on this stage three times. Twice with you and once with Lucas and never with Mitchell. This time, I get to have all my Doms together for the first time."

"It's what you want and it's what you need, too," he told her.

She smiled. "It is."

"You respond to each of us differently."

"Yes, Sir."

He glanced over at Lucas and Mitchell. They were almost finished setting up the scene. "Tell me what you're feeling, sub."

"Truthfully, Master, I feel like a virgin again. I've never been with more than one man at a time. I know that sounds weird, being a girl from Destiny, but it's true."

He touched her cheek. "No, baby, that's not weird at all. In fact, I'm glad you haven't. My brothers and I shared you emotionally, claiming you as our girl, but never physically. I blame that on timing, our military service, college, and how busy we all were, but the truth is we were young and inexperienced. We weren't ready. Tonight, we are. Mitchell, Lucas, and I want to claim you for our own. This is the ultimate sharing. You are ours, Phoebe Blue. All ours."

"Yes, Master. I am yours."

He crushed his mouth to her juicy lips. "Thank you, baby."

"For what?"

"For saving me."

"You saved me, too, Jason."

He walked her to the bench, where Lucas and Mitchell stood on opposites sides.

The three of them helped her lie face down on the bench.

"Let me put my hands behind my back, Sirs. That way you can put them in the cuffs."

He grinned. He loved her fire. "We give the orders, sub." He tugged on her hair, reminding her who was in charge. "You will obey our every command. Understand?"

"Yes, Master," she whispered in a sweet tone of submissiveness he loved.

He stroked her neck. "We're going to cuff your hands forward to the legs of the bench, baby. That way we can have free access to this beautiful back." He ran his fingers up and down her spine and was rewarded with a tremble from her.

They placed her wrists and ankles in cuffs and attached them to the D-clamps on the legs of the bench.

The hubbub of the crowd was growing.

Jason bent down, looking into her blue eyes seeing several glimmers of excitement. "You're gorgeous, baby."

"Thank you, Master. You are, too."

He'd never been called gorgeous before, but hearing it from her trembling lips thrilled him. "You're mine, baby, mine and my brothers."

* * * *

Attached to the bench, Phoebe could barely hold back her excitement. "Yes, Sir. I'm yours, Lucas, and Mitchell's submissive."

Jason bent down and kissed her long and deep.

The *oohs* and *ahs* she heard from the onlookers gave her a nice tingle in her belly. She loved every shiver of anticipation inside her. Pride swelled in her chest, wearing her three Wolfe brother's collar in front of the Phase Four crowd. With the lighting at the club, she could only make out silhouettes but no faces.

"Don't move." Jason's command froze her in place. "Very good." He straightened up and turned to their audience. "Time to take your seats."

I'm going to actually do this? My bottom is going to be bare in front of everyone?

Mitchell came up beside her. "Focus on only us, honey."

God, he was so sweet, so loving. "Yes, Sir. I will." The fantasy of being on display on one of the stages at Phase Four was about to become a reality for her. But it was more than her exhibitionist's desires that was making her so very hot. It was that her three men, her three Doms, wanted to show her off, and that filled her with pride and even more desire.

Mitchell and Lucas caressed her as Jason continued instructing the crowd with what his expectations were for them.

Always in charge. Always a Dom.

A few asked questions, as Mitchell and Lucas inspected cuffs holding her ankles and wrists to the bench.

"Don't forget, we are in charge," Lucas reminded her. "Trust us. That's all we want from you."

A shiver ran up and down her spine. "Yes, Sir. I won't forget."

She recalled how they'd told her the scene would play out tonight. The first part would be filled with all kinds of delicious torments to her ass. Bare hands. Paddles. Crops. All kinds of wicked lovelies. Her nipples and clit began to throb just thinking about it.

"Let's begin." Jason's words sounded like the gunshot.

She felt his hands on her waist, his fingers gently raking her bare flesh between the skirt and top. Her skin tingled and her body shook as his hands moved from her hips to her ass along her thighs. When he tugged her skirt up, exposing her bare ass, she felt heat flood her cheeks.

Her heart thrummed in her chest. *No panties. My ass is completely exposed.*

She felt his big hands cup her bottom.

"Always inspect your sub's ass, especially if you have played recently. See how perfect my sub's..."

As he continued giving instructions to the crowd, she tried to keep from smiling. The pride for her in every one of Jason's syllables couldn't be missed, and that filled her with such joy.

"...and I like to keep her guessing. Surprises in play can have excellent results. Lucas, demonstrate that for us."

"My pleasure," Lucas said.

"And her pleasure, too." Jason's tone elated her.

Lucas placed a blindfold on her, and the room, the club, the crowd, even the world, disappeared from her sight.

Jason continued, "Mitchell, you're up."

"Ready, bro." Mitchell placed something right between her legs. *This wasn't part of the plan.* Her breath caught in her chest when she heard a click and the toy began to hum. *A vibrator?*

Unable to hold back, she moaned, feeling her pussy's response to the oscillations.

"As you can see, our sub wasn't expecting this. Keeping things unpredictable is just one of the tools Doms can use to get their subs into the desired state."

Lucas kissed her ear. "Don't come until we tell you." His tone held an authoritative note she'd never heard before.

"I'll try not to, Sir."

"Don't just try. Obey," Lucas commanded. "You will do as I say. You are mine."

A ball of heat rolled through her at his forceful, possessive words. *I'm his. I'm all of theirs.*

Mitchell raised the vibrator's speed, its pulses on her pussy making her so very wet and wanton. *How can I keep myself from climaxing?*

"Come, get a closer look." Jason patted her ass.

She tensed. Was he inviting other Doms up on the stage? Was this another one of their detours? She couldn't bear anyone else's hands on her body. Her lips vibrated, her safe word at the back of her throat.

Mitchell removed the vibrator. "Jason? One second."

"Folks, I need to check in with my sub," Jason told the crowd.

"Honey, hang on," Lucas said, his loving tone back in place.

Clearly, they'd sensed the sudden shiver of hesitation in her. All three of her men seemed to be able to read her like an open book. They would never lead her wrong.

Jason bent down and said quietly, "No one will touch you but your three Doms. Trust me."

"I do. I trust all three of you." Her heart continued to beat so very fast. Excited, she was ready to go down any path of his, Lucas's, and Mitchell's choosing. "Thank you, Master."

"We can stop this now. Just say the word."

Her heart soared. God, he always knew her better than she knew herself. "I'm fine, Master."

"Damn right, you're fine. Fine as they come, sub. Time to show you off to these Doms. You're the diamond they only wish they could have, but they can't. You are my prize, baby. Mine and my brothers." Jason tugged on her hair and began addressing the crowd again.

You are mine, too, Jason Wolfe. Mine.

She heard the boots of Doms walking up on stage. They came so close, but none ever touched her. Still, knowing the eyes of so many were getting an unobstructed view of her ass was adding to her delicious dizziness. For the first time in her life, she didn't feel self-conscious about her body. Pride ran through her from the top of her head to the bottom of her toes and everywhere in between. Her guys saw her as beautiful, and that made her feel beautiful.

The only fingers on her skin were Jason's, Lucas's, and Mitchell's, their caresses causing her flesh to tingle and burn deliciously.

Jason's words seemed so far off, though he was so very close, the heat of his breath warming her.

"Color protocol, sub. *Green, yellow, red.* You're safe word can be either *red* or the word you and we three know." He grabbed her ass with his big manly hands and squeezed. "Understand?"

"Yes, Master. I understand."

She knew that at any time she wanted to communicate to her Doms that she was nearing a limit she could say *yellow. Red* was another safe word, though she would choose to say the one they'd agreed on long ago, should she need to. But deep down, she didn't think she would. She trusted the Wolfes with her pleasure. They knew her better than anyone.

Simultaneously, the brothers touched her. Jason smacked her ass with his bare hand. Mitchell shoved the vibrator between her legs. Lucas tweaked her nipples. The stinging pleasure sent her mind and body spinning. The pressure continued to build inside.

"Do not come," Lucas ordered. "I will let you know when you can, understand?"

She nodded, though wondering how she would keep herself from going over the edge into blissful release. She closed her eyes, trying to slow her breathing. Not possible.

Jason's slaps to her ass came faster and stung hotter.

Whack. Whack. Whack.

Mitchell pressed the vibrator to her swollen, wet pussy, making her clit throb like mad.

Buzz. Buzz. Buzz.

Lucas continued tweaking her nipples and tugging on her hair.

Her moans could not be held back as they slipped out of her mouth and through her lips.

Suddenly, her three Doms stopped right at the point she was about to climax. How had they known she was about to give in to her desire and come? They seemed to know and sense everything in her.

"Color, sub?" Jason asked.

"I am green, Master."

Lucas took off the blindfold. He smiled. "My turn."

His two little words made her even wetter.

Although she couldn't see him, she knew something sensual was going to happen. She felt something flat and cool touch her ass. *A paddle.*

"Count for me, sub," Lucas ordered.

Anxiously excited, she answered, "Yes, Sir."

Mitchell removed the vibrator and began playing with her clit. She needed relief so badly.

Thwack. The wicked toy landed in the very middle of her ass, delivering a stinging sensation that got her even hotter.

"One, Sir."

Thwack. Thwack. Thwack. "Two. Three. Four." How she was able to say it, she had no idea. The last slap to her ass sent her into that dreamy state of surrender she loved so very much.

She got even wetter as Lucas sent the paddle to her bottom again and again while Mitchell fingered her pussy, sending a couple of his digits deep into her.

"Five. Six. Seven."

Instinct kicked in, and she shifted her hips, opening herself to Mitchell's fingers, trying to reach that spot that would give the relief her body demanded.

Another rain of slaps to her ass enhanced the pressure to a breaking point. She wasn't sure she could contain herself from coming.

"Please," she whispered, unable to hold back. "Please."

"Feel good, pet?" Lucas whispered wickedly in her ear.

"Yes. God yes."

He kissed her cheek. "I can tell you want more, don't you?"

She was on fire. Her pussy ached and her clit throbbed until she thought she might pass out. "Yes, Master. Please. More."

Jason cupped her ass, which sizzled like a flame. "Time for the crop, sweetheart."

She felt him slowly drag the little monster down her back and to her ass. Suddenly, the bite of the crop burned her bottom even more than the paddle had.

Smack.

She slipped fully into that dreamy trance-like state.

"Do not come," Lucas reminded her. "Not until we give you permission."

She moaned, her need so great, her want so overwhelming.

Smack.

The wicked leathery kiss to her ass from Jason's crop, and the delicious fingers on her pussy and breasts from Mitchell's and Lucas's hands multiplied the already frenzied sensations inside her.

Lucas warned again, "Do. Not. Come."

Desperate for release, she pleaded with him, but mercy wasn't given.

"Just a little bit longer, baby," he said tenderly. "You can take more. Trust me. It will make your climax even better."

Smack. Smack. Smack.

Tears of frustration fell from her eyes. "Please let me come, Masters. Please. I beg you."

"That's what I love to hear," Lucas said. "Shall we let her?"

"Not yet," Jason said in a deep, lusty tone. "Not just yet. We are the Doms here, sub. Not you. Us."

"Oh God, Master."

"Do you feel my control over you? Do you feel Lucas's and Mitchell's power, too?"

"Yes, Master. I do."

"Do you surrender to us? Everything?"

"Yes. Yes. Yes. I surrender, Master. I surrender to you and Master Lucas and Master Mitchell. I'm yours."

"Beautiful words." His tone seemed filled with a kind of awe. "So beautiful."

"Please. Please. Please." Even though he was in control, she doubted she could hold back the overwhelming need inside her much longer. It was about to burst inside her and she didn't know how to stop it.

All three of her Doms smiled their approval.

"Now, you can come. Come for us, sub," Jason commanded. "Do it, now."

Her entire body shook, as the most intense climax she'd ever experienced released the pressure that had been building since they walked into the club. Sensations zoomed through her body as her pussy began to spasm violently.

The scene was over and she was somewhat aware of the crowd applauding. Her guys applied cream to her backside, which felt incredible. Then they removed the restraints and placed the blindfold back on her. They carried her off the stage.

When they removed the blindfold, she realized they'd taken her into one of the club's private rooms. This one had a large bed in the center of the space. Another surprise, as that had not been discussed with her prior to coming to Phase Four.

Her Doms stood in front of her, completely naked, three sexy beasts, their monstrous erections in their fists.

"Strip out of your clothes, sub." Jason's face had little expression for her to read.

Same with Mitchell and Lucas. She knew in her heart that the reason for their steely demeanor was all part of the play, keeping her on her toes.

"Yes, Master." Slipping off her skirt, she tried to catch little glances of them to get a clue as to their state of mind, but could only sense their determination and will in their eyes.

After she was completely naked, Mitchell commanded, "Bend over, sub. Grab your ankles."

She obeyed instantly.

Mitchell, her sensitive musician, somehow had been transformed into a full-on Dom tonight. Sure, he'd played at BDSM, but never had she seen him so intense. He massaged her breasts, sending several shivers through her body.

"Look at this." Lucas fingered her backside, raising her temperature. "We colored this sweet ass perfectly."

Lucas, her balanced builder, embraced his dominant side completely now.

Jason…well, Jason was being Jason—a Dom through and through.

He came up behind her. His fingers slid over her swollen folds. "Our slave's juices shouldn't go to waste."

She felt him grip her hips and spread her thighs apart. Then he buried his face between her legs, licking her pussy with his wicked tongue. He squeezed her thighs with his hands. A silent reminder that he was in control, he was in charge.

This had been her dream long ago, surrendering everything to her three men at the same time.

He slid his tongue through her swollen, wet folds. "God, your cream tastes so sweet."

When he sucked on her clit, she moaned and balled up her hands as the pressure grew and grew. "Mmm."

"I like the sound coming from this pretty mouth." Mitchell ran his fingers over her vibrating lips. "I can only imagine what she's thinking right now."

Think? I can't think about anything right now with Jason drinking from my pussy, Lucas fingering my ass, and Mitchell massaging my breasts.

"I can't wait to make love to our sub." Lucas's words were laden with deep, hot lust. "Would you like that, pet?"

"Yes. Please. I beg you."

"That's what I enjoy hearing. There will be more of that tonight. You'll see."

The pressure began to build again, faster and hotter than before.

Jason's delicious oral assault ended suddenly, and she instantly missed his mouth on her pussy. "I'm going to plug this ass. Get it ready for my cock. What do you think about that, baby?"

"I'm excited, Master," she confessed.

Jason applied lubricant to her ass and began stretching her out with his fingers. "Color, sub?"

"Green, Sir," she answered. *So very, very green.*

She felt him drag the toy on her ass's flesh, still burning from the scene they'd run in the other room. When he sent the tip of it past her anus, she held her breath. The deeper in, the wider the spread of her flesh. The last thrust by Jason had it slip into her ass until the tapered bases locked it into place, causing her toes to curl.

"I'm going to leave that in for a bit, sub." He tapped on the handle, sending a vibration through her body. "Once I know you deserve it, I'm going to claim your ass with my cock."

"Please, Master. Please."

Mitchell placed a dildo at her lips. "Suck this, baby. Show us what your hot mouth can do to a dick."

She parted her lips and swallowed the head of the toy.

Mitchell grabbed her hand and placed it on his cock. "I'm a lot bigger than this dildo. I want to fuck your mouth. Practice makes perfect, baby. That's what they say. Prove to me that you can take my cock. Show me."

She took more of the dildo down her throat, hoping to impress him with her skills.

"Very good, baby," Mitchell said, removing the toy. "Straighten up."

"Yes, Master." When she stood upright, the plug shifted slightly, causing her to tremble. A ball of need swirled in her belly, moving to her core and settling in her pussy, which was aching like mad.

"Time for some electric play on these," Lucas said, tweaking her taut nipples. "She's never enjoyed the violet wand before. I wonder what our pretty little pet thinks about that."

She saw the purple glass electrode in his hand, causing her to shiver wonderfully. His smile made him look devilishly handsome. When he placed the tip of the wand on her arm, she felt a little, tickling bite.

"Just a taste. Let's turn it up a bit, baby." The next kiss of the wand hit her nipple and she squealed with delight.

Back and forth Lucas sent the wand to her taut buds until she was shrieking and getting even wetter. He crouched down in front of her. "Don't move."

"I'll try, Sir," she stammered out, realizing what he clearly meant to do with the wand. But she trusted him with all her heart. All three of these wonderful men were her Doms, but more than that, they were going to be her husbands, too.

"Don't just try, sub." Lucas pressed the toy to her pussy for a split second, and she yelped but didn't move. "Nice, baby. Very nice."

Another zap to her sex caused her to chew on her lower lip.

Lucas moved the wand down her thighs and back up to her pussy, dotting her flesh with electric kisses.

"Oh God. Please. Please. I need you, Masters. I need to feel you inside my body."

Lucas ran his hand up and down her back. "You are so beautiful when you beg, baby. We are going to make you feel so good."

She felt Jason remove the plug from her ass.

Mitchell lifted her into his muscled body. She wrapped her arms around his neck.

She saw Lucas get on the bed, face up.

"We're going to claim you as ours, sweetheart." Mitchell sent his mouth to hers, and she parted her lips slightly in surrender. When he released her mouth, he continued, "Together. At the same time. We planned this, baby. For you. How do you feel about that?"

"It's been my dream, Sir." Her body burned to be filled by her men.

He lowered her down into Lucas's waiting arms.

Lucas kissed her deeply, causing her lips to throb, which sent a line of want straight to her pussy and clit. She could feel his thick, hard cock pressing on her swollen folds, which only multiplied her need to be filled by them. She felt as if she would go mad if they didn't get inside her soon.

"Spread your legs," Lucas commanded in a growl.

Hearing his rumbling tone rising up from his chest took her breath away. He was pure masculine heat, and she felt so very feminine in his embrace.

She parted her legs as wide as possible.

Lucas smiled. "That's my girl."

God, that sounded so right. *His girl, his, Mitchell's and Jason's.* This was so right. Being here with him, with Mitchell, with Jason. This was where she belonged. They would be her husbands. With them, she would start a family. Her eyes welled up with happy tears.

Lucas's face tightened suddenly. "Phoebe, are you all right?"

What a question. For three years, living without her Wolfe men, she'd suffered such long, lonely nights. Her entire world had been crushed, her heart broken.

"I'm more than all right," she told him. "I love you, Lucas." She said his name. Had to, even though she knew it was breaking protocol. Her heart was overflowing with so many emotions for him, for Mitchell, and for Jason.

Lucas kissed her again, his lips and tongue possessing her mouth utterly. "I love you, baby. I will never let you go. Ever. Trust me about that."

"I do," she said.

He thrust his cock into her pussy, the friction adding to her immense growing pressure.

Mitchell cupped her chin, positioning himself until his dick was right in front of her face. His cock was a monster, thick and long. "I love you, Phoebe. I love you so much."

"I love you." In her mind, she could hear the sound, Mitchell's sound—*our sound.* She took hold of his dick. "I want to taste you."

He smiled. "I can't wait to feel your lips on me."

Waiting wasn't going to be possible for long, with Lucas filling her pussy with his cock. She was getting so close. Anxious for more, she licked the manly drop from the tip of Mitchell's dick.

"Time for this gorgeous ass to be filled up completely. This toy isn't sufficient for the task. It was only getting you ready for my cock, pet." Jason's lips caressed the middle of her back, causing her to shiver. "I love you."

"I love you, Jason."

He climbed on top of her body, his weight pinning her to Lucas.

Jason thrust his dick into her ass, causing her breath to catch for a moment in her chest. Her need surged and her breathing returned, though coming in pants and gasps.

"I'm yours," she confessed breathlessly before swallowing Mitchell's cock.

She burned so hot with her men. They stretched and filled her to the very core of her being. Having them all inside her body was just what she longed for, and now it was happening.

Lucas groaned. "She's close, and so am I."

"I'm so close, too. God, she's sucking me into madness." Mitchell moaned, stroking her hair. "God, so fucking close."

Jason's breathing was labored. "Come for us, baby."

Yes, Master.

Their thrusts sent her over the edge into a pleasure-filled sea of their making.

Everything inside her exploded into a myriad of sensations, each one new and more powerful than the one before.

In and out, their cocks went into her pussy, ass, and mouth. Her Doms were dominating her completely. This was what she'd dreamed of for so long. Being with them. Together.

I'm theirs.

Overwhelming emotions flooded her entire being. Surrounded by her men, she felt her heart swell.

She was joined once again to them. Entwined with them. Renewed by them. Her world exploded with every color of the rainbow.

She rode the wave, thrashing between them.

Her pussy clenched tight on Lucas, as did her ass on Jason.

She hollowed out her cheeks, sucking on Mitchell, who came first, sending his seed down her throat.

She drank every drop.

She felt Lucas swell inside her, his thrusts coming faster and faster. His eyes narrowed and his lips parted when he sent his cock deep into her pussy.

"Fuuuck." Jason released inside her ass.

Her entire body shook violently. She writhed between her Doms like a live wire, hot and electric.

Her men kissed and caressed her everywhere. She moaned, feeling completely sated.

"I love you, sweetheart." Lucas smiled, sending her to the moon.

Mitchell stroked her hair. "I love you, baby."

Jason kissed her on the back of the neck. "I love you, Phoebe.

You are mine. You are ours."

Together, her three men had made love to her, claiming her as their own for all time.

She'd pushed Jason, Lucas, and Mitchell away as hard as she could three years ago, but her men had never given up on her. They'd worked their way back into her heart, choosing her once again, letting go of the past and forgiving all her mistakes.

She'd grown up with them in Destiny. Now, she was finally home.

"I love you, my three wonderful Doms."

Chapter Twenty

Sitting in Blue's Diner with Shane and Corey, Jason finished his breakfast. "Guys, your parents make the best food in the entire state."

"I agree, bro." Shane looked like the epitome of health. It was so good to see his friend back on his feet. "I'm shocked that I'm not five hundred pounds."

Belle White walked through the front door to the diner with Juan and the other boys from the ranch.

Seeing how Shane and Corey reacted whenever Belle was near put a smile on Jason's face.

They were totally into her.

Being so happy and in love with Phoebe, he wanted the same for his friends.

"Have you two asked her on a date yet?"

"Not yet," Corey answered. "My brother is just now back to normal."

Shane smiled. "I'm far from normal, right, Jason?"

He laughed. "You're telling me. Get off your lazy asses and ask her out."

They both grinned.

"Where are your fiancée and your two brothers, Jason?" Shane asked. "It's rare to see you without them these days."

"Hard for any of us to be away from our baby too long," he admitted freely. The four of them had been almost inseparable since finally coming together at Phase Four two nights before. "They're back at the house. I had some paperwork at the office to do early this morning. They are supposed to meet me here in about ten minutes.

We're going to the florist with Phoebe to help her pick out flowers for the wedding."

He couldn't wait to marry her. The future had never seemed brighter.

"I'm sure Phoebe's got all three of you knee-deep in the wedding planning," Shane said. "The only part I would like would be the cake tasting at the diner. Mom makes the best cakes."

Phoebe walked into the restaurant with Lucas and Mitchell.

She was smiling, which filled him with joy.

Tonight they were going to have her take a pregnancy test.

She was only a week late, which she told them did happen sometimes. But he could sense something different in her.

God, I hope she's pregnant.

He and his brothers were ready to be dads, and he knew Phoebe would make a wonderful mother.

"Hi, honey," she said, leaning over and giving Jason a kiss.

"Hey, baby." He scooted over and she slid in next to him.

Lucas and Mitchell pulled over a couple of chairs from an empty table.

"Good to see you up and around, Shane," Lucas said.

"Good to be up and around, too. I'm ready for some good old-fashioned dragon hunting. How about you guys? I think it would be fun to take Juan and the other boys next weekend. Are you game?"

"I am," Mitchell chimed in.

"Wait a second." Phoebe shook her head.

"Something wrong, sis?" Shane asked.

"You just got released by Doc. It's too soon for you to ride a horse or hike in the mountains."

"That's just the point. I have been released." Shane grabbed her hands. "You should be more concerned about your wedding than about me. I can take care of myself."

"When's the date you tie the knot?" Corey grinned. "I've checked the *Destiny Daily* and haven't seen anything published about it yet."

"April 12th," Shane said. "I know. I'm the best man."

"When were you guys planning on telling the other groomsmen?" Corey teased. "We need to know, too."

Phoebe smiled. "You two seem pretty excited about my wedding."

"They are, baby. That's all they've been talking about this morning with me." Jason turned to Shane and Corey. "Maybe you should worry about your own love life and go talk to Belle."

"No time like the present." Shane slid out of the booth.

Corey nodded and did the same.

Before they took a single step Belle's direction, Jason got a message on his ROC.

"Hold on, fellows." He pulled out the device that Brown had given him.

The team's ROCs had been recalibrated by Matt, Sean, and Jena so that Kip wouldn't be able to hack in again. Agent Black congratulated them on the new security saying it was being implemented throughout the CIA's network.

Black's sudden appearance from the grave had shocked and thrilled Brown. Turned out the two had worked together on a couple of missions a year ago.

Black was the senior agent of the team now, with Brown reporting to him.

Shannon's Eight been renamed to Shannon's Elite. New agents would be coming to Destiny soon.

"Maybe Lunceford has been found," Shane said, pulling out his own ROC.

God, I hope so.

At least Destiny was a little safer now that Mitrofanov was gone. That battle was finally over.

The next battle was about to begin. Kip Lunceford had declared war on Destiny.

With Shane and the rest of Shannon's Elite by his side, Jason believed they would bring the psycho down.

He stared at his screen.

It was a message from Black.

Just learned that Lunceford has a sister.

Intel says she's headed to Destiny.

THE END

WWW.CHLOELANG.COM

ABOUT THE AUTHOR

Chloe Lang began devouring romance novels during summers between college semesters as a respite to the rigors of her studies. Soon, her lifelong addiction was born, and to this day, she typically reads three or four books every week.

For years, the very shy Chloe tried her hand at writing romance stories, but shared them with no one. After many months of prodding by an author friend, Sophie Oak, she finally relented and let Sophie read one. As the prodding turned to gentle shoves, Chloe ultimately did submit something to Siren-BookStrand. The thrill of a life happened for her when she got the word that her book would be published.

For all titles by Chloe Lang, please visit
www.bookstrand.com/chloe-lang

Siren Publishing, Inc.
www.SirenPublishing.com

CPSIA information can be obtained at www.ICGtesting.com
Printed in the USA
LVOW10s2107101214

418177LV00022B/1095/P